I0763244

Sherlock Holmes – A Study in Illustrations

A Collection of Early Illustrations from various publications

Volume ll

With Sidney Paget now in our rear-view mirror, we have a number of interesting illustrators ahead of us in this volume

Michael J. Foy

All characters appearing in this work are fictitious, any resemblance to real persons, living or dead. The opinions expressed herein are those of the authors and not of MX Publishing.

Paperback ISBN 978-1-78705-925-2

Published by MX Publishing
335 Princess Park Manor, Royal Drive,
London, N11 3GX
www.mxpublishing.com

Cover design by Brian Belanger

Foreword

Well, I did say that Sidney Paget was in the rear-view mirror, but as they say, 'Objects in the Mirror are closer than they appear', and with that in mind we have to include a few Paget illustrations (87 in fact) to show the similarity of his work to our featured Mysterious unsigned Artist'[1]. Some might consider this as being a bit sneaky, you might say that ' you are paying again for images that have already appeared in volume 1', 'Michael is recycling old Paget images to pad out his new book', Indeed, the very thought of that! I have just included them to illustrate just how close some of these images are to the work of Paget (The unsigned Artist is assumed to be Richard Gutschmidt). Now, while it is true that all the duplicated Paget images have appeared in Volume 1, please note that you are getting a new image on each shared page and while the first book was 398 pages, this book is over 450 and the Paget images haven't added to the page count, so think of these repeated Pagets as a nice Bonus. {I promise no Paget images in at least Volume 3. (The first colour volume)}

So, who else do we have in this volume, well as previously mentioned we have 228 Richard Gutschmidt illustrations(maybe), and some Arthur Twidle, a few Graham Grinham, then George Hutchinson, Richard Pallier and finally Thomas Jeffs Nicholl.

Alexis Barquin has helped tremendously with my compilation of this book and you really must visit his Sir Arthur Conan Doyle website at www.arthur-conan-doyle.com for all things Doyley or is that Doyly? (I know it's not Doily)

Feedback is ALWAYS welcome, and changes are made when I screw things up, which happens regularly. Please contact me if you can share any light on the unsigned artist.

Anyway, enjoy the Second volume.

Did I mention volume 3 is the much awaited colour one. (lovely)

Mike Foy, Florida.
please contacted me at SherlockHolmesImages@gmail.com

---

[1] A big Thank you to Alexis Barquin's for his research work, I had guessed that these 'Russian' images were produced by Richard Gutschmidt, they had his style, and there were some unsigned images in the 9 volume German set which Richard Gutschmidt had contributed to, so I may be wrong and if I have maligning RG, I humbly apologise, and will amend further editions. So if you can prove me wrong, please let me know.

Index

Grinham, Graham **242**
Red-Headed League, The 249
Scandal in Bohemia, A 248
Sign of the Four, The 247
Study in Scarlet, A 243

Gutschmidt, Richard **6**
Abbey Grange, The 236
Beryl Coronet, The 104
Black Peter 213
Blue Carbuncle, The 86
Boscombe Valley Mystery, The 74
Cardboard Box, The 119
Case of Identity, A 71
Charles Augustus Milverton 216
Copper Beeches, The 108
Crooked Man, The 142
Dancing Men, The 204
Empty House, The 198
Engineer's Thumb, The 96
Final Problem, The 163
Five Orange Pips, The 78
Gloria Scott, The 130
Gold Pince-Nez, The 228
Greek Interpreter, The 151
Hound of the Baskervilles, The 1905 168
Man with the Twisted Lip, The 81
Missing Three-Quarter, The 232
Musgrave Ritual, The 133
Naval Treaty, The 154
Noble Bachelor, The 100
Norwood Builder, The 201
Priory School, The 210
Red-Headed League, The 67
Reigate Squires, The 137
Resident Patient, The 146
Scandal in Bohemia, A 62
Second Stain, The 239
Sign of Four, The 1904 38
Silver Blaze 113
Six Napoleons, The 221
Solitary Cyclist, The 207
Speckled Band, The 91
Stockbroker's Clerk, The 126
Study in Scarlet, A 1902 15
Study in Scarlet, A 1902 Part 1 14
Study in Scarlet, A 1902 Part 2 28
Three Students, The 224
Yellow Face, The 123

Hutchinson, George Wylie ... **250**
Study in Scarlet, A ... 251

Nicholl, Thomas Jeffs ... **311**
Sign of the Four, The ... 312

Pallier, Raymond ... **345**
Hound of the Baskervilles, The (1/19). 23rd Oct 1921 ... 346
Hound of the Baskervilles, The (2/19). 30th Oct 1921 ... 353
Hound of the Baskervilles, The (3/19). 6th Nov 1921 ... 360
Hound of the Baskervilles, The (4/19). 13th Nov 1921 ... 367
Hound of the Baskervilles, The (5/19). 20th Nov 1921 ... 371
Hound of the Baskervilles, The (6/19). 27th Nov 1921 ... 376
Hound of the Baskervilles, The (7/19). 4th Dec 1921 ... 381
Hound of the Baskervilles, The (8/19). 11th Dec 1921 ... 386
Hound of the Baskervilles, The (9/19). 18th Dec 1921 ... 391
Hound of the Baskervilles, The (10/19). 25th Dec 1921 ... 396
Hound of the Baskervilles, The (11/19). 1st Jan 1922 ... 401
Hound of the Baskervilles, The (12/19). 8th Jan 1922 ... 407
Hound of the Baskervilles, The (13/19). 15th Jan 1922 ... 413
Hound of the Baskervilles, The (14/19). 22nd Jan 1922 ... 419
Hound of the Baskervilles, The (15/19). 29th Jan 1922 ... 424
Hound of the Baskervilles, The (16/19). 5th Feb 1922 ... 429
Hound of the Baskervilles, The (17/19). 12th Feb 1922 ... 435
Hound of the Baskervilles, The (18/19). 19th Feb 1922 ... 440
Hound of the Baskervilles, The (19/19). 26th Feb 1922 ... 446

Twidle, Arthur ... **293**
Bruce-Partington Plans, The December 1908 ... 305
Study in Scarlet, A 1903 ... 294
Wisteria Lodge September 1908 ... 295

Richard Gutschmidt

Born Neuruppin 1861,

Died Munich 1926

Richard Gutschmidt was a German Painter, illustrator and graphic artist. As a student, from 1884 until 1891, he studied under Ludwig von Herterich at the academy of Arts in Munich. Using his skills as a painter and illustrator, the illustrated German editions of detective novels, by Anna Katharine Green and more importantly for us anyway, Sir Arthur Conan Doyle. He was a member of the Munich Artists' associations and the Luitpold group.

He was the first German Sherlock Holmes artist and illustrated 40 Sherlock Holmes stories, producing 228 images, spanning the years from 1902 up to 1908. These were printed in Stuttgart, Germany, by the publisher Robert Lutz. In addition, 76 of the same illustrations appeared unsigned in two Russian books. Never let it be said that Richard Gutschmidt wasn't inspired by Sidney Paget, in fact there are no Sherlock Holmes Gutschmidt drawings after the last Paget one, (in The Second Stain), were they perhaps the same person, well, no actually, Gutschmidt died 4 years before Paget.

Maybe it's a bit unfair to show Paget and Gutschmidt drawings side by side so that you can see just how 'inspired' Gutschmidt was, but who said life was fair. Just remember the first two Holmes stories were never illustrated by Paget, Gutschmidt's 'A Study in Scarlet' and 'The Sign of Four' are uniquely Gutschmidtesque. So here is the Gutschmidt collection of illustrations. Any 'Pagetised' illustrations will be shown next to the original Paget image, otherwise Gutschmidt gets a full page to himself. The work will be in Canon order as are the reference numbers rather than published dates, which are all over the place as some of the stories are out of order and in completely the 'wrong' volumes. Let's deal with the German nine volume set in the following table before we look at the two Russian books. Gutschmidt knew the old saying "If you must copy an image, copy from the very best" Richard Gutschmidt was a very talented artist.

The German publisher, Robert Lutz printed 9 books set of Sir Arthur Conan Doyle's stories mainly the earlier Sherlock Holmes ones, between 1902 and 1908 in Stuttgart.

Vol.	Year	Stories	Title	Illustrations
1	1902	1	Späte Rache Late Revenge - (A Study in Scarlet)	24
2	1902	1	Das Zeichen der Vier (The sign of the four)	24
3	1902	7	Der Bund der Rothaarigen und andere Detektivgeschichten (The Red-headed League and other detective stories)	30
4	1902	6	Das getupfte Band und andere Detektivgeschichten (The Speckled Band and other detective stories)	28
5	1902	7	Fünf Apfelsinenkerne und andere Detektivgeschichten (Five Orange Pips and other detective stories)	35
6	1903	1	Der Hund von Baskerville (The Hound of the Baskervilles)	30
7	1905	7	Als Sherlock Holmes aus Lhassa kam sieben Neue Detektivgeschichten (Seven new Sherlock Holmes stories after Lhassa)	22
8	1906	6	Die tanzenden Männchen und andere Detektivgeschichten (The Dancing men and other detective stories)	18
9	1908	7	Sherlock Holmes und die Ohren nebst anderen Geschichten Sherlock Holmes and the ears among other stories	17

Volumes 1,2 and 6 contained three of the four Novellas, while the other volumes had the short stories but not in Canon order.

Here is a breakdown of the collection, with a comment on whether the story appeared in either of the Russian books.

Volume 1 Contents of Späte Rache (1902, Robert Lutz) 24 illustrations

German Title	English Title	Ill.	Russian
Späte Rache	A Study in scarlet	24	N

So that one is easy Canon Story 1. (See table at back of book for Canon numbers).

Volume 2 Contents of Das Zeichen der Vier (1902, Robert Lutz) 24 illustrations

German Title	English Title	Ill.	Russian
Das Zeichen der Vier	The Sign of the Four	24	N

So far so good with Story 2.

Volume 3 Seven stories from Der Bund der Rothaarigen und andere Detektivgeschichten 1902

No.	German Title	English Title	Ill.	Russian
1	Der Bund der Rothaarigen	The Red-Headed League	4	Y
2	Eine Skandal-geschichte im Fürstentum O...	A Scandal in Bohemia	5	Y
3	Ein Fall Geschickter Täuschung	A Case of Identity	3	Y
4	Der Geheimnisvolle Mord im Thale von Boscombe	The Boscombe Valley Mystery	4	Y
5	Eine Sonderbare Anstellung	The Stockbroker's Clerk	4	Y
6	Der Mann mit der Schramme	The Man with the Twisted Lip	5	Y
7	Die Geschichte des Blauen Karfunkels	The Blue Carbuncle	5	Y

Bit of a mix up here with Stories 4, 3, 5, 6, 18, 8 and 9, but fear not all of the first 40 stories up to The Second Stain are going to be covered.

Volume 4 Six stories from Das getupfte Band und andere Detektivgeschichten 1902

No.	German Title	English Title	Ill.	Russian
1	Das Getupfte Band	The Speckled Band	5	Y
2	Der Daumen des Ingenieurs	The Engineer's Thumb	4	Y
3	Die Verschwundene Braut	The Noble Bachelor	4	Y
4	Die Geschichte des Beryll-Kopfschmuckes	The Beryl Coronet	4	Y
5	Das Landhaus in Hampshire	The Copper Beeches	5	Y
6	Silberstrahl	Silver Blaze	6	Y

Starting the teenage Stories 10, 11, 12, 13, 14 &15.

Volume 5 Seven stories from Fünf Apfelsinenkerne und andere Detektivgeschichten 1902

No.	German Title	English Title	Ill.	Russian
1	Fünf Apfelsinenkerne	The Five Orange Pips	3	N
2	Der Katechismus des Familie Musgrave	The Musgrave Ritual	4	N
3	Die Gutsherren von Reigate	The Reigate Squires	5	N
4	Der Krüppel	The Crooked Man	4	N
5	Der Doktor und sein Patient	The Resident Patient	5	N
6	Der Marinevertrag	The Naval Treaty	9	N
7	Das letzte Problem	The Final Problem	5	N

Covering most of the twenties we have Stories 7, 20, 21, 22, 23, 25 & 26

Volume 6 Contents of Der Hund von Baskerville 1903

German Title	English Title	Ill.	Russian
Der Hund von Baskerville	The Hound of the Baskervilles	30	N

Story 27 on its own, but it is a big one.

Volume 7 Seven stories from Als Sherlock Holmes aus Lhassa kam sieben Neue Detektivgeschichten 1905

No.	German Title	English Title	Ill.	Russian
1	Im Leeren Hause	The Empty House	3	N
2	Der Baumeister von Norwood	The Norwood Builder	3	N
3	Das Gelbe Gesicht	The Yellow Face	3	N
4	Der Griechische Dolmetscher	The Greek Interpreter	3	N
5	Holmes' Erstes Albenteuer	The Gloria Scott	3	N
6	Der Golden Klemmer	The Gold Pince-Nez	4	N
7	Die Einsame Radfahrerin	The Solitary Cyclist	3	N

Middle age ones follow next with Stories 28, 29, 17, 24, 19, 37 & 31

Volume 8 Seven stories from Die tanzenden Männchen und andere Detektivgeschichten 1906

No.	German Title	English Title	Ill.	Russian
1	Die tanzenden Männchen	The Dancing Men	3	Y
2	Die Entführung aus der Klosterschule	The Priory School	3	Y
3	Die Schwarze Peter	Black Peter	3	Y
4	Die Sechs Napoleonbüsten	The Six Napoleons	3	Y
5	Der Mord im Abbey Grange	The Abbey Grange	3	Y
6	Der Zweite Blutflecken	The Second Stain	3	Y

Jumping to the end of the series with Stories 30, 32, 33, 35, 39 & 40.

Volume 9 had four stories from Sherlock Holmes und die Ohren nebst anderen Geschichten 1908

No.	German Title	English Title	Ill.	Russian
1	Sherlock Holmes und die Ohren	The Cardboard Box	4	Y
2	Sherlock Holmes als Einbrecher	Charles Augustus Milverton	5	Y
3	Die drei Studenten	The Three Students	4	Y
4	Der vermißte Fußballspieler	The Missing Three-Quarter	4	Y

And finally, 16, 34, 36 & 38 as well as some non-Sherlock Holmes stories (not included) and the job is complete.

Unsigned Richard Gutschmidt drawings from the Russian books.

Maybe because there wasn't a German book for 1904, and Gutschmidt wanted some income that year, his illustrations were published without his name in a couple of Russian books. In 1904, Two Sherlock Holmes books were published in Russia, One in Moscow and the other in St. Petersburg. The Moscow book was called the Adventures of Sherlock Holmes (**Приключения Шерлока Холмса**) and had 112 pages. It appears that this book was composed of two volumes Volume 2 was dated 3rd March 1904 and had 80 pages, I shall refer to these works as Book 1 and Book 2.

Book 1 was a collection of the following 5 stories with a total of 20 illustrations	
The Speckled Band -	5 illustrations
The Engineer's Thumb –	4 illustrations
The Noble Bachelor –	4 illustrations
The Beryl Coronet –	4 illustrations
The Copper Beeches –	3 illustrations

Book 2 contained a collection of 3 stories	17 Sidney Page illustrations
The Empty House –	5 illustrations
The Dancing Men –	5 illustrations
Black Peter –	7 illustrations

The St. Petersburg's book called Adventures of the detective Sherlock Holmes (**Приключенческий сыщика Шерлок Холмс**) had 346 pages and had the following 13 stories. There were a total of 56 illustrations

The redheaded league –	4 illustrations
A Scandal in Bohemia –	3 illustrations
The Case of Identity –	3 illustrations
The Boscombe Valley Murder –	4 illustrations
The Stockbroker's Clerk -	4 illustrations
The Man with the Twisted Lip –	5 illustrations
The Blue Carbuncle –	5 illustrations
The Speckled Band –	5 illustrations
The Engineer's Thumb –	4 illustrations
The Noble Bachelor –	4 illustrations
The Beryl Coronet –	4 illustrations
The Copper Beeches –	5 illustrations
Silver Blaze –	6 illustrations

Приключения Шерлока Холмса
Москва 1904
And
Приключенческий сыщика Шерлок Холмс
С. Петербург 1904
Adventures of Sherlock Holmes
Moscow 1904 and St. Petersburg. 1904

		Illustrations and Pages					
	Illustration-St. Petersburg	1	2	3	4	5	6
1	REDH	6	14	23	27		
2	SCAN	33	37	56			
3	IDEN	61	67	75			
4	BOSC	88	91	99	104		
5	STOC	114	123	125	129		
6	TWIS	135	141	144	148	155	
7	BLUE	162	168	177	181	184	
8	SPEC	188	193	198	206	209	
9	ENGR	216	220	226	231		
10	NOBL	244	248	257	260		
11	BERY	268	273	281	289		
12	COPP (5 illustrations)	295	308	313	316	321	
13	SILV	326	328	331	336	339	344

		Illustrations						
	Illustration-Moscow	1	2	3	4	5	6	7
1	SPEC	4	9	12	15	21		
2	ENGR	41	46	48	52			
3	NOBL	60	64	70	72			
4	BERY	78	81	85	90			
5	COPP (3 illustrations)	95	100	105				
6	EMPT – Paget	7	9	15	19	22		
7	DANC – Paget	29	35	45	51	53		
8	BLAC – Paget	57	63	65	68	69	76	78

Please note that two of Richard Gutschmidt's illustrations for The Copper Beeches that were included in the St. Petersburg printing were missing in the Moscow book.

More information regarding the Sidney Paget illustrations that were used in The Empty House, The Dancing Men and Black Peter. Refer to Volume 1 for the images.

		Illustrations						
	Illustration-Moscow	1	2	3	4	5	6	7
6	EMPT – Page	7	9	15	19	22		
	Vol. 1 Page	P296	P297	P298	P299	P301		
	SP No.	SP263	SP264	SP265	SP266	SP368		
7	DANC – Page	29	35	45	51	53		
	Vol. 1 Page	P310	P312	P315	P309	P316		
	SP No.	SP277	SP278	SP281	SP276	SP282		
8	BLAC – Page	57	63	65	68	69	76	78
	Vol. 1 Page	P335	P336	P337	P338	P334	P339	P340
	SP No.	SP300	SP301	SP302	SP303	SP299	SP304	SP305

So, let's get started with the full Richard Gutschmidt Sherlock Holmes' illustrations in strict Canon order, starting with A Study in Scarlet and working our way through to the Second Stain. It's nice to see Watson's Army career shown in illustration 1 as well as young Stamford in 2.

Richard Gutschmidt – A Study in Scarlet
1902

Vol.1 -Späte Rache

Part 1, Chapter 1. *Mr. Sherlock Holmes*

Image 1/24. I should have fallen into the hands of the murderous Ghazis had it not been for the devotion and courage shown by Murray, my orderly.

Ref. SH-RG1

Richard Gutschmidt – A Study in Scarlet 1902

Vol.1 -Späte Rache

Part 1, Chapter 1. *Mr. Sherlock Holmes*

Image 2/24. "I've found it! I've found it," he shouted to my companion.
Ref. SH-RG2

Richard Gutschmidt – A Study in Scarlet 1902
Vol.1 -Späte Rache
Part 1, Chapter 2. *The Science of Deduction*

Image 3/24. Leaning back in his armchair of an evening, he would close his eyes and scrape carelessly at the fiddle which was thrown across his knee.
Ref. SH-RG3

Richard Gutschmidt – A Study in Scarlet 1902
Vol.1 -Späte Rache
Part 1, Chapter 2. *The Science of Deduction*

Image 4/24. "For Mr. Sherlock Holmes," he said.
Ref. SH-RG4

Richard Gutschmidt – A Study in Scarlet 1902

Vol.1 -Späte Rache

Part 1, Chapter 3. The Lauriston Garden Mystery

Image 5/24. My attention was centred upon the single, grim, motionless figure which lay stretched upon the boards.
Ref. SH-RG5

Richard Gutschmidt – A Study in Scarlet 1902

Vol.1 -Späte Rache

Part 1, Chapter 3. The Lauriston Garden Mystery

Image 6/24. "Look at that!" He said, triumphantly.

Ref. SH-RG6

Richard Gutschmidt – A Study in Scarlet 1902

Vol.1 -Späte Rache

Part 1, Chapter 4. What John Rance Had to Tell

Image 7/24. The door was decorated with a small slip of brass on which the name Rance was engraved.
Ref. SH-RG7

Richard Gutschmidt – A Study in Scarlet 1902
Vol.1 -Späte Rache
Part 1, Chapter 4. What John Rance Had to Tell

Image 8/24. “I’ve seen many a drunk chap in my time,” he said, “but never anyone so cryin’ drunk as that cove.”
Ref. SH-RG8

Richard Gutschmidt – A Study in Scarlet 1902
Vol.1 -Späte Rache
Part 1, Chapter 5. Our Advertisement Brings a Visitor

Image 9/24. A very old and wrinkled woman hobbled into the apartment.
Ref. SH-RG9

Richard Gutschmidt – A Study in Scarlet 1902

Vol.1 -Späte Rache

Part 1, Chapter 6. Tobias Gregson Shows What He Can Do

Images 10/24. “Have you found it, Wiggins?”

Ref. SH-RG10

Richard Gutschmidt – A Study in Scarlet 1902

Vol.1 -Späte Rache

Part 1, Chapter 6. Tobias Gregson Shows What He Can Do

Image 11/24. Lestrade stood in the centre of the room, fumbling nervously with his hat and uncertain what to do.

Ref. SH-RG11

Richard Gutschmidt – A Study in Scarlet 1902

Vol.1 -Späte Rache

Part 1, Chapter 7. Light in the Darkness

Image 12/24. The dog continued to lie stretched upon the cushion.
Ref. SH-RG12

Richard Gutschmidt – A Study in Scarlet 1902

Vol.1 -Späte Rache

Part 1, Chapter 7. Light in the Darkness

Image 13/24 So powerful and so fierce was he that the four of us were shaken off again and again.

Ref. SH-RG13

Richard Gutschmidt – A Study in Scarlet 1902

Vol.1 -Späte Rache

Part 2, Chapter 1. On the Great Alkali Plain

Image 14/24 “You’ve got to put your hands up like this. It makes you feel kind of good.”

Ref. SH-RG14

Richard Gutschmidt – A Study in Scarlet 1902

Vol.1 -Späte Rache

Part 2, Chapter 1. On the Great Alkali Plain

Image 15/24 One of the rescue party seized the little girl and hoisted her upon his shoulder.

Ref. SH-RG15

Richard Gutschmidt – A Study in Scarlet 1902
Vol.1 -Späte Rache
Part 2, Chapter 2. The Flower of Utah

Image 16/24 A sinewy brown hand caught the frightened horse by the curb.
Ref. SH-RG16

Richard Gutschmidt – A Study in Scarlet 1902

Vol.1 -Späte Rache

Part 2, Chapter 2. The Flower of Utah

Image 17/24 “It is settled, then. The longer I stay, the harder it will be to go.”
Ref. SH-RG17

Richard Gutschmidt – A Study in Scarlet 1902

Vol.1 -Späte Rache

Part 2, Chapter 3. John Ferrier talks with the Prophet

Image 18/24 “It were better for you, John Ferrier,” he thundered, “that you and she were now lying blanched skeletons upon the Sierra Blanco, than that you should put your weak wills against the orders of the holy four!”

Ref. SH-RG18

Richard Gutschmidt – A Study in Scarlet 1902
Vol.1 -Späte Rache
Part 2, Chapter4 A Flight for Life

Image 19/24 He saw to his astonishment a man lying flat upon his face upon the ground.
Ref. SH-RG19

Richard Gutschmidt – A Study in Scarlet 1902

Vol.1 -Späte Rache

Part 2, Chapter 4 A Flight for Life

Image 20/24 'Nine to seven,' cried the sentinel.

Ref. SH-RG20

Richard Gutschmidt – A Study in Scarlet 1902
Vol.1 -Späte Rache
Part 2, Chapter 5. The Avenging Angels

Image 21/24 "John Ferrier, formerly of Salt Lake City. Died August 4th, 1860."
Ref. SH-RG21

Richard Gutschmidt – A Study in Scarlet 1902

Vol.1 -Späte Rache

Part 2, Chapter 6. A Continuation of the Reminiscences of John Watson, M.D.

Image 22/24 "I've got a good deal to say," our prisoner said slowly.

Ref. SH-RG22

Richard Gutschmidt – A Study in Scarlet 1902

Vol.1 -Späte Rache

Part 2, Chapter 6. A Continuation of the Reminiscences of John Watson, M.D.

Image 23/24. “He gazed at me with bleared, drunken eyes for a moment, and then I saw a horror spring up in them, and convulse his whole features, which showed me that he knew me.”

Ref. SH-RG23

Richard Gutschmidt – A Study in Scarlet 1902
Vol.1 -Späte Rache
Part 2, Chapter 7. The Conclusion

Image 24/24. "Didn't I tell you so when we started?" Cried Sherlock Holmes with a laugh.
Ref. SH-RG24

Richard Gutschmidt – The Sign of Four 1904
Vol.2 -Das Zeichen der Vier
Chapter 1. *The Science of Deduction*

Image 1/24. His eyes rested thoughtfully upon the sinewy forearm and wrist.
Ref. SH-RG25

Richard Gutschmidt – The Sign of Four 1904

Vol.2 -Das Zeichen der Vier

Chapter 1. *The Science of Deduction*

Image 2/24. He balanced the watch in his hand.

Ref. SH-RG26

Richard Gutschmidt – The Sign of Four 1904

Vol.2 -Das Zeichen der Vier

Chapter 2. *The Statement of the Case*

Image 3/24. 'State your case,' said he in brisk business tones.
Ref. SH-RG27

Richard Gutschmidt – The Sign of Four 1904

Vol.2 -Das Zeichen der Vier

Chapter 3. *In Quest of a Solution*

Image 4/24. A small, dark, brisk man in the dress of a coachman

Ref. SH-RG28

Richard Gutschmidt – The Sign of Four 1904

Vol.2 -Das Zeichen der Vier

Chapter 4. *The Story of the Bald-Headed Man*

Image 5/24. 'I will tell you how Morstan died,' he continued.
Ref. SH-RG29

Richard Gutschmidt – The Sign of Four 1904

Vol.2 -Das Zeichen der Vier

Chapter 5. *The Tragedy of Pondicherry Lodge*

Image 6/24. A short, deep-chested man stood in the opening.

Ref. SH-RG30

Richard Gutschmidt – The Sign of Four 1904
Vol.2 -Das Zeichen der Vier
Chapter 5. *The Tragedy of Pondicherry Lodge*

Image 7/24. In a wooden armchair the master of the house was seated all in a heap, with his head sunk upon his left shoulder and that ghastly, inscrutable smile upon his face.
Ref. SH-RG31

Richard Gutschmidt – The Sign of Four 1904

Vol.2 -Das Zeichen der Vier

Chapter 6. *Sherlock Holmes Gives a Demonstration*

Image 8/24. He held down the lamp to the floor.

Ref. SH-RG32

Richard Gutschmidt – The Sign of Four 1904

Vol.2 -Das Zeichen der Vier

Chapter 6. *Sherlock Holmes Gives a Demonstration*

Image 9/24. 'Mr. Sholto, it is my duty to inform you that anything which you may say will be used against you.

Ref. SH-RG33

Richard Gutschmidt – The Sign of Four 1904

Vol.2 -Das Zeichen der Vier

Chapter 7. *The Episode of the Barrel*

Image 10/24. A friend of Mr. Sherlock is always welcome,' said he

Ref. SH-RG34

Richard Gutschmidt – The Sign of Four 1904

Vol.2 -Das Zeichen der Vier

Chapter 7. *The Episode of the Barrel*

Image 11/24. We had been following the guidance of Toby.
Ref. SH-RG35

Richard Gutschmidt – The Sign of Four 1904

Vol.2 -Das Zeichen der Vier

Chapter 8. *The Baker Street Irregulars*

Image 12/24. 'Dear little chap!' said Holmes strategically

Ref. SH-RG36

Richard Gutschmidt – The Sign of Four 1904

Vol.2 -Das Zeichen der Vier

Chapter 8. *The Baker Street Irregulars*

Image 13/24. And away they buzzed down the stairs.
Ref. SH-RG37

Richard Gutschmidt – The Sign of Four 1904
Vol.2 -Das Zeichen der Vier
Chapter 9. *A Break in the Chain*

Image 14/24. ‘I am off down the river, Watson.’
Ref. SH-RG38

Richard Gutschmidt – The Sign of Four 1904

Vol.2 -Das Zeichen der Vier

Chapter 9. *A Break in the Chain*

Image 15/24. ‘Here is the old man,’ said he, holding out a heap of white hair.
Ref. SH-RG39

Richard Gutschmidt – The Sign of Four 1904

Vol.2 -Das Zeichen der Vier

Chapter 10. *The End of the Islander*

Image 16/24. The furnaces roared, and the powerful engines whizzed and clanked like a great metallic heart.

Ref. SH-RG40

Richard Gutschmidt – The Sign of Four 1904

Vol.2 -Das Zeichen der Vier

Chapter 10. *The End of the Islander*

Image 17/24. Our pistols rang out together.

Ref. SH-RG41

Richard Gutschmidt – The Sign of Four 1904
Vol.2 -Das Zeichen der Vier
Chapter 11. *The Great Agra Treasure*

Image 18/24. He sat now with his handcuffed hands upon his lap.
Ref. SH-RG42

Richard Gutschmidt – The Sign of Four 1904

Vol.2 -Das Zeichen der Vier

Chapter 11. *The Great Agra Treasure*

Image 19/24. 'Then I say "Thank God," too.'

Ref. SH-RG43

Richard Gutschmidt – The Sign of Four 1904
Vol.2 -Das Zeichen der Vier
Chapter 12. *The Strange Story of Jonathan Small*

Image 20/24. Broke away across the paddy-fields.
Ref. SH-RG44

Richard Gutschmidt – The Sign of Four 1904
Vol.2 -Das Zeichen der Vier
Chapter 12. *The Strange Story of Jonathan Small*

Image 21/24. In an instant the two Sikhs were upon me.
Ref. SH-RG45

Richard Gutschmidt – The Sign of Four 1904

Vol.2 -Das Zeichen der Vier

Chapter 12. *The Strange Story of Jonathan Small*

Image 22/24. And close at his heels, bounding like a tiger, the great black-bearded Sikh, with a knife flashing in his hand.

Ref. SH-RG46

Richard Gutschmidt – The Sign of Four 1904

Vol.2 -Das Zeichen der Vier

Chapter 12. *The Strange Story of Jonathan Small*

Image 23/24. 'I want you just to let Captain Morstan hear that story from your own lips, Small,' said he.

Ref. SH-RG47

Richard Gutschmidt – The Sign of Four 1904

Vol.2 -Das Zeichen der Vier

Chapter 12. *The Strange Story of Jonathan Small*

Image 24/24. ‘I am much obliged to you both for your assistance.’

Ref. SH-RG48

Richard Gutschmidt - A Scandal in Bohemia

Vol.3 Der Bund der Rothaarigen und andere Detektivgeschichten 1902.

& St. Petersburg Book 1904

SCAN: Image 1.

Sidney Paget
The Strand, July 1891

SH-SP1. Sidney Paget Original.
"Then he stood before the fire."

German P. 57
St. Petersburg P. 33

Image 1/5

Ref. SH-RG49

Richard Gutschmidt - A Scandal in Bohemia

Vol.3 Der Bund der Rothaarigen und andere Detektivgeschichten 1902.
& St. Petersburg Book 1904
SCAN: Image 2.

Sidney Paget
The Strand, July 1891

German Vol.3 P. 63
& St. Petersburg P. 37

SH-SP3. Sidney Paget Original.
"A man entered."

Image 2/5.
Ref. SH-RG50

Richard Gutschmidt - A Scandal in Bohemia

Vol.3 Der Bund der Rothaarigen und andere Detektivgeschichten 1902.

& St. Petersburg Book 1904

SCAN: Image 3.

Sidney Paget
The Strand, July 1891

SH-SP6. Sidney Paget
Original. "I found myself
mumbling responses."

German Vol.3 P.79

Image 3/5.

Ref. SH-RG51

Richard Gutschmidt - A Scandal in Bohemia

Vol.3 Der Bund der Rothaarigen und andere Detektivgeschichten 1902.

& St. Petersburg Book 1904

SCAN: Image 4.

Sidney Paget
The Strand, July 1891

SH-SP7. Sidney Paget
Original. “A simple minded clergyman.”

German Vol.3 P. 84

Image 4/5.

Ref. SH-RG52

Richard Gutschmidt - A Scandal in Bohemia

Vol.3 Der Bund der Rothaarigen und andere Detektivgeschichten 1902.

& St. Petersburg Book 1904

SCAN: Image5.

Sidney Paget
The Strand, July 1891

SH-SP10. Sidney Paget
Original. “This Photograph.”

German Vol. 3 P.97
St. Petersburg P.56

Image 5/5.

Ref. SH-RG53

Richard Gutschmidt – The Red-Headed League

Vol.3 Der Bund der Rothaarigen und andere Detektivgeschichten 1902.

& St. Petersburg Book 1904

REDH: Image 1.

Sidney Paget
The Strand, August 1891

SH-SP12. Sidney Paget
Original.
"What on earth does this mean?"

German Vol.3 P.12
St. Petersburg P.6

Image 1/4.

Ref. SH-RG54

Richard Gutschmidt – The Red-Headed League

Vol.3 Der Bund der Rothaarigen und andere Detektivgeschichten 1902.

& St. Petersburg Book 1904

REDH: Image 2.

Sidney Paget
The Strand, August 1891

German Vol.3 P. 26
& St. Petersburg P. 14

SH-SP15. Sidney Paget Original.
"The door was shut and locked?"

Image 2/4
Ref. SH-RG55

Richard Gutschmidt – The Red-Headed League

Vol.3 Der Bund der Rothaarigen und andere Detektivgeschichten 1902.

& St. Petersburg Book 1904

REDH: Image 3.

Sidney Paget
The Strand, August 1891

German Vol.3 P. 41
& St. Petersburg P. 23

SH-SP19. Sidney Paget Original. "Mr. Merryweather stopped to light a lantern."

Image 3/4
Ref. SH-RG56

Richard Gutschmidt – The Red-Headed League

Vol.3 Der Bund der Rothaarigen und andere Detektivgeschichten 1902.

& St. Petersburg Book 1904

REDH: Image 4.

Sidney Paget
The Strand, August 1891

SH-SP20. Sidney Paget
Original.
"It's no use, John Clay."

German Vol.3 P.12
St. Petersburg P.27

Image 4/4.

Ref. SH-RG57

Richard Gutschmidt - A Case of Identity

Vol.3 Der Bund der Rothaarigen und andere Detektivgeschichten 1902.

& St. Petersburg Book 1904

IDEN: Image 1.

Sidney Paget
The Strand, September 1891

SH-SP21. Sidney Paget Original. "Sherlock Holmes welcomed her."

German Vol.3 P.104
St. Petersburg P.61

Image 1/3.

Ref. SH-RG58

Richard Gutschmidt - A Case of Identity

Vol.3 Der Bund der Rothaarigen und andere Detektivgeschichten 1902.

& St. Petersburg Book 1904

IDEN: Image 2.

Sidney Paget.
The Strand, September 1891

SH-SP23. Sidney Paget Original. “There was no one there.”

German Vol.3 P.63
St. Petersburg P.67

Image 2/3

Ref. SH-RG59

Richard Gutschmidt - A Case of Identity

Vol.3 Der Bund der Rothaarigen und andere Detektivgeschichten 1902.

& St. Petersburg Book 1904

IDEN: Image 3.

Sidney Paget.
The Strand, September 1891

SH-SP26. Sidney Paget
Original.
"Glancing about him like a rat in a trap."

German Vol.3 P.104
St. Petersburg P.75

Image 3/3.

Ref. SH-RG60

Richard Gutschmidt – The Boscombe Valley Mystery

Vol.3 Der Bund der Rothaarigen und andere Detektivgeschichten 1902.

& St. Petersburg Book 1904

BOSC: Image 1.

Sidney Paget.
The Strand, October 1891

German Vol.3 P.141
& St. Petersburg P.88

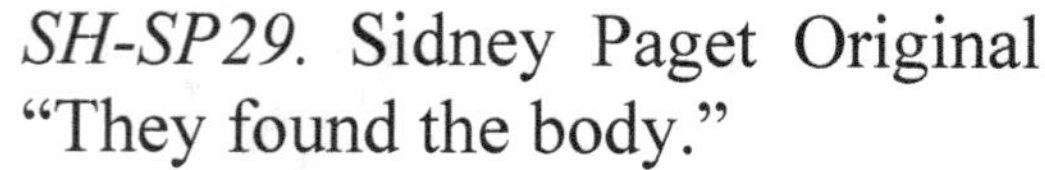

SH-SP29. Sidney Paget Original.
"They found the body."

Image 1/4.
Ref. SH-RG61

Richard Gutschmidt – The Boscombe Valley Mystery

Vol.3 Der Bund der Rothaarigen und andere Detektivgeschichten 1902.

& St. Petersburg Book 1904

BOSC: Image 2.

Sidney Paget.
The Strand, October 1891

SH-SP31. Sidney Paget Original. "Lestrade shrugged his shoulders."

German Vol.3 P.155
& St. Petersburg P.91

Image 2/4.

Ref. SH-RG62

Richard Gutschmidt – The Boscombe Valley Mystery

Vol.3 Der Bund der Rothaarigen und andere Detektivgeschichten 1902.

& St. Petersburg Book 1904

BOSC: Image 3.

Sidney Paget. The Strand, October 1891

SH-SP34. Sidney Paget Original.
“For a long time he remained there.”

German Vol.3 P.169 & St. Petersburg P.99

Image 3/4.
Ref. SH-RG63

Richard Gutschmidt – The Boscombe Valley Mystery

Vol.3 Der Bund der Rothaarigen und andere Detektivgeschichten 1902.

& St. Petersburg Book 1904

BOSC: Image 4

Sidney Paget.
The Strand, October 1891

German Vol.3 P.177
& St. Petersburg P.104

SH-SP36. Sidney Paget Original.
" 'Mr. John Turner,' said the waiter."

Image 4/4.
Ref. SH-RG64

Richard Gutschmidt – The Five Orange Pips

Vol.5 Fünf Apfelsinenkerne und andere Detektivgeschichten 1902.

FIVE: Image 1.

Sidney Paget.
The Strand, November 1891

German Vol.5 P.11

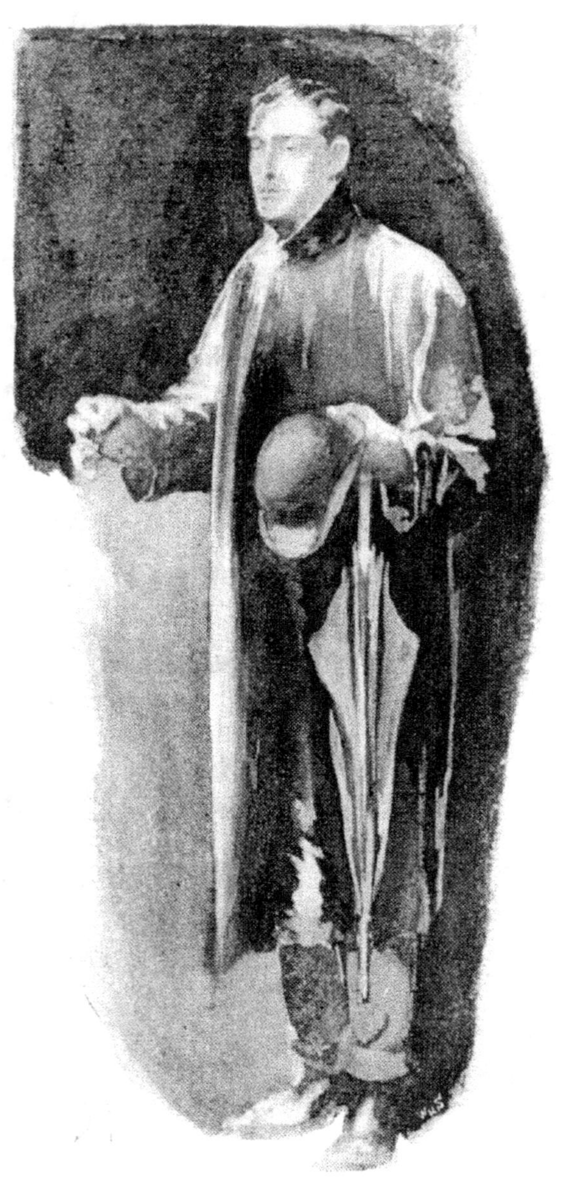

SH-SP38. Sidney Paget Original. "He looked about him anxiously."

Image 1/3.
Ref. SH-RG65

Richard Gutschmidt – The Five Orange Pips

Vol.5 Fünf Apfelsinenkerne und andere Detektivgeschichten 1902

FIVE: Image 2

Sidney Paget.
The Strand, November 1891

SH-SP40. Sidney Paget Original.
"What on Earth does this mean?"

German Vol.5 P.16

Image 2/3.

Ref. SH-RG66

Richard Gutschmidt – The Five Orange Pips
Vol.5 Fünf Apfelsinenkerne und andere Detektivgeschichten 1902.
FIVE: Image 3.

Sidney Paget.
The Strand, November 1891

SH-SP43. Sidney Paget Original.
“Holmes,” I cried, “You are too late.”

German Vol.5 P.36

Image 3/3.

Ref. SH-RG67

Richard Gutschmidt – The Man with the Twisted Lip

Vol.3 Der Bund der Rothaarigen und andere Detektivgeschichten 1902.

& St. Petersburg Book 1904

TWIS: Image 1.

Sidney Paget.
The Strand, December 1891

German Vol.3 P.230
& St. Petersburg P.135

SH-SP44. Sidney Paget Original.
"Staring into the fire."

Image 1/5.
Ref. SH-RG68

Richard Gutschmidt – The Man with the Twisted Lip

Vol.3 Der Bund der Rothaarigen und andere Detektivgeschichten 1902.

& St. Petersburg Book 1904

TWIS: Image 2.

Sidney Paget.
The Strand, December 1891

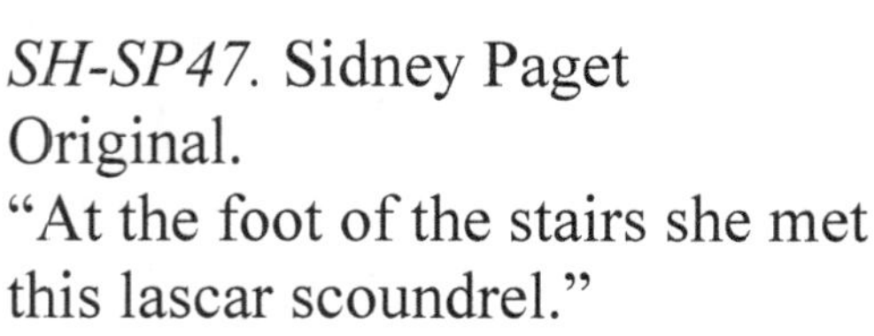

SH-SP47. Sidney Paget
Original.
"At the foot of the stairs she met this lascar scoundrel."

German Vol.3 P.241
& St. Petersburg P.141

Image 2/5.

Ref. SH-RG69

Richard Gutschmidt – The Man with the Twisted Lip

Vol.3 Der Bund der Rothaarigen und andere Detektivgeschichten 1902.

& St. Petersburg Book 1904

TWIS: Image 3

Sidney Paget.
The Strand, December 1891

SH-SP48. Sidney Paget Original.
"He is a professional beggar."

German Vol.3 P.245
St. Petersburg P.144

Image 3/5.

Ref. SH-RG70

Richard Gutschmidt – The Man with the Twisted Lip

Vol.3 Der Bund der Rothaarigen und andere Detektivgeschichten 1902.

& St. Petersburg Book 1904

TWIS: Image 4.

Sidney Paget.
The Strand,
December 1891

SH-SP50. Sidney Paget Original. " 'Frankly now,' She repeated."

German Vol.3 P.254
St. Petersburg P.148

Image 4/5.

Ref. SH-RG71

Richard Gutschmidt – The Man with the Twisted Lip

Vol.3 Der Bund der Rothaarigen und andere Detektivgeschichten 1902.

& St. Petersburg Book 1904

TWIS: Image 5

Sidney Paget.
The Strand, December 1891

SH-SP53. Sidney Paget Original. “He broke into a scream.”

German Vol.3 P.267
St. Petersburg P.155

Image 5/5.

Ref. SH-RG72

Richard Gutschmidt – The Blue Carbuncle

Vol.3 Der Bund der Rothaarigen und andere Detektivgeschichten 1902.

& St. Petersburg Book 1904

BLUE: Image 1.

Sidney Paget.
The Strand, January 1892

SH-SP54. Sidney Paget Original. “A very seedy hard felt hat.”

German Vol.3 P.277
St. Petersburg P.162

Image 1/5.

Ref. SH-RG73

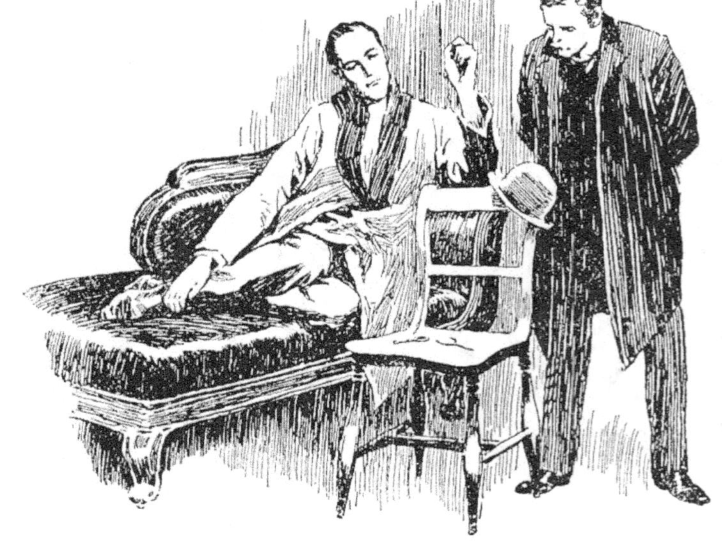

Richard Gutschmidt – The Blue Carbuncle

Vol.3 Der Bund der Rothaarigen und andere Detektivgeschichten 1902.

& St. Petersburg Book 1904

BLUE: Image 2

Sidney Paget.
The Strand, January 1892

SH-SP56. Sidney Paget Original. "See what my wife found in its crop!"

German Vol.3 P.288
St. Petersburg P.168

Image 2/5.

Ref. SH-RG74

Richard Gutschmidt – The Blue Carbuncle

Vol.3 Der Bund der Rothaarigen und andere Detektivgeschichten 1902.

& St. Petersburg Book 1904

BLUE: Image 3

Sidney Paget.
The Strand, January 1892

SH-SP58. Sidney Paget Original. "Just read it out to me."

German Vol.3 P.304
St. Petersburg P.177

Image 3/5.

Ref. SH-RG75

Richard Gutschmidt – The Blue Carbuncle

Vol.3 Der Bund der Rothaarigen und andere Detektivgeschichten 1902.

& St. Petersburg Book 1904

BLUE: Image 4.

Sidney Paget.
The Strand, January 1892

German Vol.3 P.312
St. Petersburg P.181

SH-SP60. Sidney Paget Original.
" 'Have mercy!' he shrieked."

Image 4/5.
Ref. SH-RG76

Richard Gutschmidt – The Blue Carbuncle

Vol.3 Der Bund der Rothaarigen und andere Detektivgeschichten 1902.

& St. Petersburg Book 1904

BLUE: Image 5

Sidney Paget.
The Strand, January 1892

SH-SP61. Sidney Paget Original. "He burst into convulsive sobbing."

German Vol.3 P.318
St. Petersburg P.184

Image 5/5.

Ref. SH-RG77

Richard Gutschmidt – The Speckled Band

Vol.4 Das getupfte Band und andere Detektivgeschichten 1902.

& Both Russian Books 1904

SPEC: Image 1

Sidney Paget.
The Strand, February 1892

SH-SP62. Sidney Paget Original. “She raised her veil.”

German Vol.4 P.11
Both Russian Books
Moscow P.4
St. Petersburg P.188

Image 1/5.

Ref. SH-RG78

Richard Gutschmidt – The Speckled Band

Vol.4 Das getupfte Band und andere Detektivgeschichten 1902.

& Both Russian Books 1904

SPEC: Image 2

Sidney Paget.
The Strand, February 1892

SH-SP64. Sidney Paget Original. "Her face blanched with terror."

Both editions

German Vol.4 P.21

Both Russian Books
Moscow P.9
St. Petersburg P.193

Image2/5.

Ref. SH-RG79

Richard Gutschmidt – The Speckled Band

Vol.4 Das getupfte Band und andere Detektivgeschichten 1902.

& Both Russian Books 1904

SPEC: Image 3

Sidney Paget.
The Strand, February 1892

German Vol.4 P.31
Moscow.P.12
St. Petersburg P.198

SH-SP65. Sidney Paget Original.
"Which of you is Holmes?"

Image 3/5.
Ref. SH-RG80

Richard Gutschmidt – The Speckled Band

Vol.4 Das getupfte Band und andere Detektivgeschichten 1902.

& Both Russian Books 1904

SPEC: Image 4.

Sidney Paget.
The Strand, February 1892

German Vol.4 P.47
Moscow.P.15
St. Petersburg P.206

SH-SP68. Sidney Paget Original.
"Good-Bye, and be brave."

Image 4/5.
Ref. SH-RG81

Richard Gutschmidt – The Speckled Band

Vol.4 Das getupfte Band und andere Detektivgeschichten 1902.

& Both Russian Books 1904

SPEC: Image 5

Sidney Paget.
The Strand, February 1892

SH-SP69. Sidney Paget Original.
"Holmes lashed furiously."

Both editions

German Vol.4 P.56

Both Russian Books
Moscow P.21
St. Petersburg P.209

Image 5/5.

Ref. SH-RG82

Richard Gutschmidt – The Engineer's Thumb

Vol.4 Das getupfte Band und andere Detektivgeschichten 1902.

& Both Russian Books 1904

ENGR: Image 1

Sidney Paget.
The Strand, March 1892

SH-SP71. Sidney Paget Original. "He unwound the handkerchief, and held out his hand."

Both editions

German Vol.4 P.67

Both Russian Books
Moscow P.41
St. Petersburg P.216

Image 1/4.

Ref. SH-RG83

Richard Gutschmidt – The Engineer's Thumb

Vol.4 Das getupfte Band und andere Detektivgeschichten 1902.

& Both Russian Books 1904

ENGR: Image 2

Sidney Paget.
The Strand, March 1892

German Vol.4 P.79
Moscow.P.46
St. Petersburg P.220

SH-SP74. Sidney Paget Original.
"Not a word to a soul!"

Image 2/4.
Ref. SH-RG84

Richard Gutschmidt – The Engineer's Thumb

Vol.4 Das getupfte Band und andere Detektivgeschichten 1902.

& Both Russian Books 1904

ENGR: Image 3

Sidney Paget.
The Strand, March 1892

German Vol.4 P.86
Moscow.P.48
St. Petersburg P.226

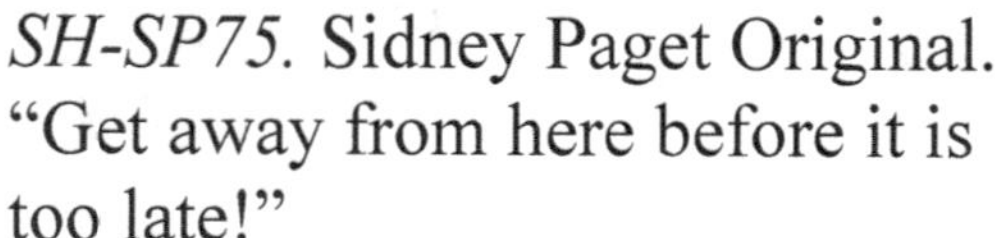

SH-SP75. Sidney Paget Original.
"Get away from here before it is too late!"

Image 3/4
Ref. SH-RG85

Richard Gutschmidt – The Engineer's Thumb

Vol.4 Das getupfte Band und andere Detektivgeschichten 1902.

& Both Russian Books 1904

ENGR: Image 4

Sidney Paget.
The Strand, March 1892

German Vol.4 P.96
Moscow.P.52
St. Petersburg P.231

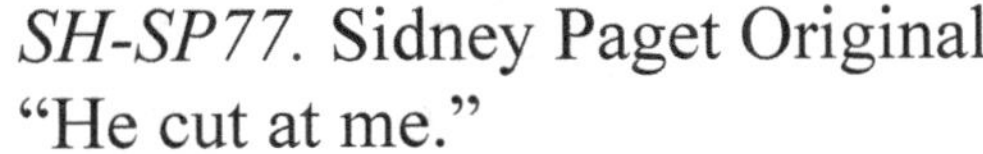

SH-SP77. Sidney Paget Original
"He cut at me."

Image 4/4.
Ref. SH-RG86

Richard Gutschmidt – The Noble Bachelor

Vol.4 Das getupfte Band und andere Detektivgeschichten 1902.

& Both Russian Books 1904.

NOBL: Image 1

Sidney Paget.
The Strand, April 1892

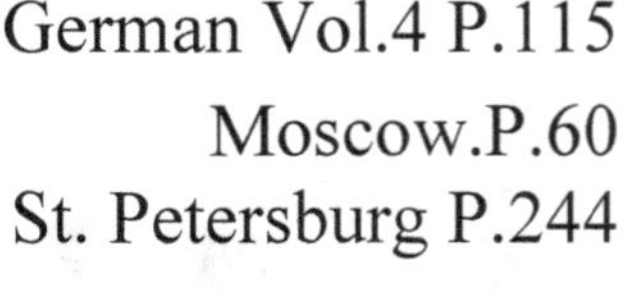

German Vol.4 P.115
Moscow.P.60
St. Petersburg P.244

SH-SP80. Sidney Paget Original. "She was ejected by the butler and the footman."

Image 1/4.
Ref. SH-RG87

Richard Gutschmidt – The Noble Bachelor

Vol.4 Das getupfte Band und andere Detektivgeschichten 1902.

& Both Russian Books 1904

NOBL: Image 2

Sidney Paget.
The Strand, April 1892

German Vol.4 P.123
Moscow.P.64
St. Petersburg P.248

SH-SP82. Sidney Paget Original. "The gentleman in the pew handed it up to her."

Image 2/4.
Ref. SH-RG88

Richard Gutschmidt – The Noble Bachelor

Vol.4 Das getupfte Band und andere Detektivgeschichten 1902.

& Both Russian Books 1904

NOBL: Image 3

Sidney Paget.
The Strand, April 1892

SH-SP84. Sidney Paget Original.
"A picture of offended dignity."

Both editions

German Vol.4 P.137

Both Russian Books
Moscow P.70
St. Petersburg P.257

Image 3/4

Ref. SH-RG89

Richard Gutschmidt – The Noble Bachelor

Vol.4 Das getupfte Band und andere Detektivgeschichten 1902.

& Both Russian Books 1904

NOBL: Image 4

Sidney Paget.
The Strand, April 1892

German Vol.4 P.143
Moscow.P.72
St. Petersburg P.260

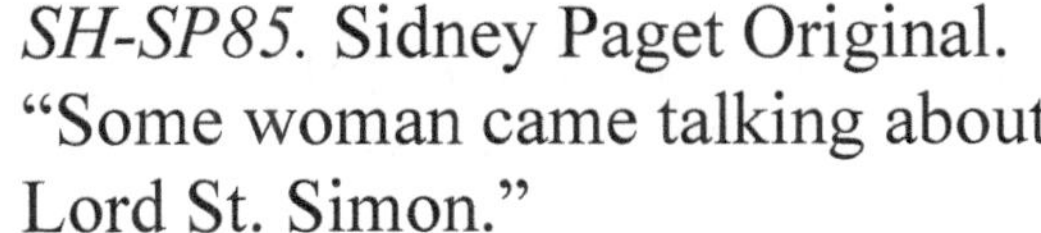

SH-SP85. Sidney Paget Original.
"Some woman came talking about Lord St. Simon."

Image 4/4.
Ref. SH-RG90

Richard Gutschmidt – The Beryl Coronet

Vol.4 Das getupfte Band und andere Detektivgeschichten 1902.

& Both Russian Books 1904

BERY: Image 1

Sidney Paget.
The Strand, May 1892

German Vol.4 P.158
Moscow.P.78
St. Petersburg P.268

SH-SP88. Sidney Paget Original.
"I took the precious case."

Image 1/4.
Ref. SH-RG91

Richard Gutschmidt – The Beryl Coronet

Vol.4 Das getupfte Band und andere Detektivgeschichten 1902.

& Both Russian Books 1904

BERY: Image 2

Sidney Paget.
The Strand, May 1892

German Vol.4 P.169
Moscow.P.81
St. Petersburg P.273

SH-SP90. Sidney Paget Original.
"At my cry he dropped it.

Image 2/4.
Ref. SH-RG92

Richard Gutschmidt – The Beryl Coronet

Vol.4 Das getupfte Band und andere Detektivgeschichten 1902.

& Both Russian Books 1904

BERY: Image 3

Sidney Paget.
The Strand, May 1892

German Vol.4 P.181
Moscow.P.85
St. Petersburg P.281

SH-SP92. Sidney Paget Original.
"Something like fear sprang up
in the young lady's eyes.

Image 3/4.
Ref. SH-RG93

Richard Gutschmidt – The Beryl Coronet

Vol.4 Das getupfte Band und andere Detektivgeschichten 1902.

& Both Russian Books 1904

BERY: Image 4

Sidney Paget.
The Strand, May 1892

German Vol.4 P.195
Moscow.P.90
St. Petersburg P.289

SH-SP94. Sidney Paget Original.
"Arthur caught him."

Image 4/4.
Ref. SH-RG94

Richard Gutschmidt – Copper Beeches

Vol.4 Das getupfte Band und andere Detektivgeschichten 1902.

& Both Russian Books 1904

COPP: Image 1

Sidney Paget.
The Strand, June 1892

SH-SP96. Sidney Paget Original. "Taking up a glowing cinder with the tongs."

Both editions

German Vol.4 P.206

Both Russian Books
Moscow P.95
St. Petersburg P.295

Image 1/5.

Ref. SH-RG95

Richard Gutschmidt – Copper Beeches

Vol.4 Das getupfte Band und andere Detektivgeschichten 1902.

& Both Russian Books 1904

COPP: Image 2

Sidney Paget.
The Strand, June 1892

SH-SP98. Sidney Paget Original. "Holmes shook his head gravely."

Both editions

German Vol.4 P.221

Both Russian Books
Moscow P.100
St. Petersburg P.308

Image 2/5.

Ref. SH-RG96

Richard Gutschmidt – Copper Beeches

Vol.4 Das getupfte Band und andere Detektivgeschichten 1902.

& Both Russian Books 1904

COPP: Image 3

Sidney Paget.
The Strand, June 1892

German Vol.4 P.239
Moscow.P.105
St. Petersburg P.313

SH-SP101. Sidney Paget Original.
"I took it up and examined it.

Image 3/5.
Ref. SH-RG97

Richard Gutschmidt – Copper Beeches

Vol.4 Das getupfte Band und andere Detektivgeschichten 1902.

& Both Russian Books 1904

COPP: Image 4

Sidney Paget.
The Strand, June 1892

German Vol.4 P.244
St. Petersburg P.316

SH-SP102. Sidney Paget Original.
" 'Oh! I am so frightened!' I panted."

Image 4/5.
Ref. SH-RG98

Richard Gutschmidt – Copper Beeches

Vol.4 Das getupfte Band und andere Detektivgeschichten 1902.

& Both Russian Books 1904

COPP: Image 5

Sidney Paget.
The Strand, June 1892

SH-SP103. Sidney Paget
Original.
“ ‘You villain!' said he,
'where's your daughter?’ ”

German Vol.4 P.253
St. Petersburg P.321

Image 5/5.

Ref. SH-RG99

Richard Gutschmidt – Silver Blaze

Vol.4 Das getupfte Band und andere Detektivgeschichten 1902.

& St. Petersburg Book 1904 .

SILV: Image 1

Sidney Paget.
The Strand, December 1892

SH-SP105. Sidney Paget Original. “Holmes gave me a sketch of the events.”

German Vol.4 P.263

St. Petersburg P.326

Image 1/6.

Ref. SH-RG100

Richard Gutschmidt – Silver Blaze

Vol.4 Das getupfte Band und andere Detektivgeschichten 1902.

& St. Petersburg Book 1904

SILV: Image 2

Sidney Paget.
The Strand, December 1892

German Vol.4 P.244
St. Petersburg P.328

SH-SP106. Sidney Paget Original.
"A man appeared out of the darkness."

Image 2/6.
Ref. SH-RG101

Richard Gutschmidt – Silver Blaze

Vol.4 Das getupfte Band und andere Detektivgeschichten 1902.

& St. Petersburg Book 1904

SILV: Image 3

Sidney Paget.
The Strand, December 1892

German Vol.4 P.272
St. Petersburg P.331

SH-SP107. Sidney Paget Original. "They found the dead body of the unfortunate trainer."

Image 3/6.
Ref. SH-RG102

Richard Gutschmidt – Silver Blaze

Vol.4 Das getupfte Band und andere Detektivgeschichten 1902.

& St. Petersburg Book.

SILV: Image 4

Sidney Paget.
The Strand, December 1892

German Vol.4 P.286
St. Petersburg P.336

SH-SP109. Sidney Paget Original.
"'Have you found them?' she panted."

Image 4/6.
Ref. SH-RG103

Richard Gutschmidt – Silver Blaze

Vol.4 Das getupfte Band und andere Detektivgeschichten 1902.

& St. Petersburg Book 1904

SILV: Image 5

Sidney Paget.
The Strand, December 1892

German Vol.4 P.294
St. Petersburg P.339

SH-SP110. Sidney Paget
Original. "Be off!"

Image 5/6.
Ref. SH-RG104

Richard Gutschmidt – Silver Blaze

Vol.4 Das getupfte Band und andere Detektivgeschichten 1902.

& St. Petersburg Book 1904

SILV: Image 6

Sidney Paget.
The Strand, December 1892

German Vol.4 P.306
St. Petersburg P.344

SH-S112. Sidney Paget Original.
"He laid his hand upon the glossy neck."

Image 6/6.
Ref. SH-RG105

Richard Gutschmidt – The Cardboard Box

Vol.9 Sherlock Holmes und die Ohren nebst anderen Geschichten 1908
CARD: Image 1

Image 1/4. We all sat down while Holmes examined, one by one, the articles which Lestrade had handed to him.

Ref. SH-RG106

Richard Gutschmidt – The Cardboard Box

Vol.9 Sherlock Holmes und die Ohren nebst anderen Geschichten 1908

CARD: Image 2

Image 2/4. “Oh, I am weary of questions!” Cried Miss Cushing impatiently.

Ref. SH-RG107

Richard Gutschmidt – The Cardboard Box

Vol.9 Sherlock Holmes und die Ohren nebst anderen Geschichten 1908

CARD: Image 3

Image 3/4. "He held out his hands quietly enough for the darbies."

Ref. SH-RG108

Richard Gutschmidt – The Cardboard Box

Vol.9 Sherlock Holmes und die Ohren nebst anderen Geschichten 1908

CARD: Image 4

Image 4/4. "I took to my heels, and I ran after the cab."

Ref. SH-RG109

Richard Gutschmidt – The Yellow Face

Vol.7 Als Sherlock Holmes aus Lhassa kam sieben Neue Detektivgeschichten

1905. P.115

YELL: Image 1

Image 1/3.

Ref. SH-RG110

Richard Gutschmidt – The Yellow Face

Vol.7 Als Sherlock Holmes aus Lhassa kam sieben Neue Detektivgeschichten

1905. P.121

YELL: Image 2

Image 2/3.

Ref. SH-RG111

Richard Gutschmidt – The Yellow Face

Vol.7 Als Sherlock Holmes aus Lhassa kam sieben Neue Detektivgeschichten

1905. P.135

YELL: Image 3

Image 3/3.

Ref. SH-RG112

Richard Gutschmidt – The Stockbroker's Clerk

Vol.3 Der Bund der Rothaarigen und andere Detektivgeschichten 1902.

& St. Petersburg Book 1904

STOC: Image 1

Sidney Paget.
The Strand, March 1893

German Vol.3 P.195
St. Petersburg P.114

SH-SP130. Sidney Paget Original. "Mr. Hall Pycroft, I believe?' said he."

Image 1/4.
Ref. SH-RG113

Richard Gutschmidt – The Stockbroker's Clerk

Vol.3 Der Bund der Rothaarigen und andere Detektivgeschichten 1902.

& St. Petersburg Book 1904

STOC: Image 2

Sidney Paget.
The Strand, March 1893

SH-SP132. Sidney Paget Original.
"He looked up at us."

German Vol.3 P.210
St. Petersburg P.123

Image 2/4.

Ref. SH-RG114

Richard Gutschmidt – The Stockbroker's Clerk

Vol.3 Der Bund der Rothaarigen und andere Detektivgeschichten 1902.

& St. Petersburg Book 1904

STOC: Image 3

Sidney Paget.
The Strand, March 1893

German Vol.3 P.214
St. Petersburg P.125

SH-SP133. Sidney Paget Original. "We found ourselves in the inner room."

Image 3/4.

Ref. SH-RG115

Richard Gutschmidt – The Stockbroker's Clerk

Vol.3 Der Bund der Rothaarigen und andere Detektivgeschichten 1902.

& St. Petersburg Book 1904

STOC: Image 4

Sidney Paget.
The Strand, March 1893

SH-SP134. Sidney Paget Original. "Glancing at the haggard figure."

German Vol.3 P.220

St. Petersburg P.129

Image 4/4.

Ref. SH-RG116

Richard Gutschmidt – The Gloria Scott

Vol.7 Als Sherlock Holmes aus Lhassa kam sieben Neue Detektivgeschichten

1905. P.192

GLOR: Image 1

Image 1/3.

Ref. SH-RG117

Richard Gutschmidt – The Gloria Scott

Vol.7 Als Sherlock Holmes aus Lhassa kam sieben Neue Detektivgeschichten

1905. P.201

GLOR: Image 2

Image 2/3.

Ref. SH-RG118

Richard Gutschmidt – The Gloria Scott

Vol.7 Als Sherlock Holmes aus Lhassa kam sieben Neue Detektivgeschichten

1905. P.217

GLOR: Image 3

Image 3/3.

Ref. SH-RG119

Richard Gutschmidt – The Musgrave Ritual

Vol.5 Fünf Apfelsinenkerne und andere Detektivgeschichten1902.

MUSG: Image 1

Sidney Paget.
The Strand, May 1893

SH-SP144. Sidney Paget Original.
"Reginald Musgrave"

German Vol.5 P.50

Image 1/4.

Ref. SH-RG120

Richard Gutschmidt – The Musgrave Ritual

Vol.5 Fünf Apfelsinenkerne und andere Detektivgeschichten1902. P.56

MUSG: Image 2

Image 2/4.

Ref. SH-RG121

Richard Gutschmidt – The Musgrave Ritual

Vol.5 Fünf Apfelsinenkerne und andere Detektivgeschichten1902.

MUSG: Image 3

Sidney Paget.
The Strand, May 1893

SH-SP147. Sidney Paget Original.
“This was the place indicated.”

German Vol.5 P.72

Image 3/4.

Ref. SH-RG122

Richard Gutschmidt – The Musgrave Ritual

Vol.5 Fünf Apfelsinenkerne und andere Detektivgeschichten1902.

MUSG: Image 4

Sidney Paget.
The Strand, May 1893

German Vol.5 P.75

SH-SP148. Sidney Paget Original.
"It was the figure of a man."

Image 4/4.
Ref. SH-RG123

Richard Gutschmidt – The Reigate Squires

Vol.5 Fünf Apfelsinenkerne und andere Detektivgeschichten1902.

REIG: Image 1

German Vol.5 P.94

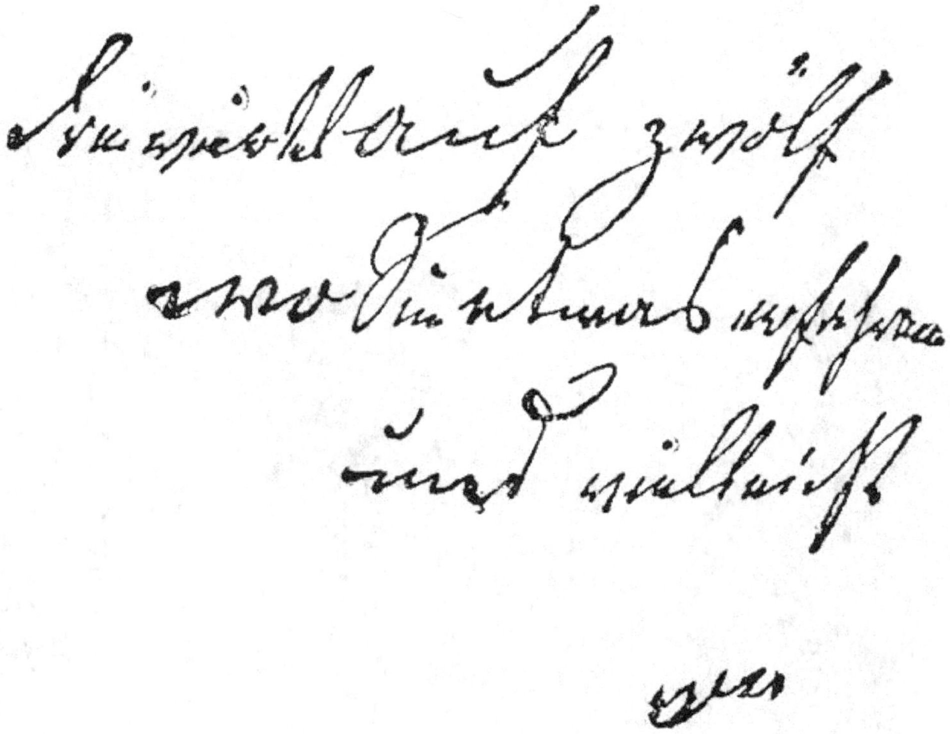

Image 1/5.

Ref. SH-RG124

Richard Gutschmidt – The Reigate Squires

Vol.5 Fünf Apfelsinenkerne und andere Detektivgeschichten1902.

REIG: Image 2

German Vol.5 P.101

Image 2/5.

Ref. SH-RG125

Richard Gutschmidt – The Reigate Squires

Vol.5 Fünf Apfelsinenkerne und andere Detektivgeschichten1902.

REIG: Image 3

Sidney Paget.
The Strand, June 1893

SH-SP152. Sidney Paget Original. “He deliberately knocked the whole thing over.”

German Vol.5 P.109

Image 3/5.

Ref. SH-RG126

Richard Gutschmidt – The Reigate Squires

Vol.5 Fünf Apfelsinenkerne und andere Detektivgeschichten1902.

REIG: Image 4

Sidney Paget.
The Strand, June 1893

SH-SP153. Sidney Paget Original.
"Bending over the prostrate figure of Sherlock Holmes."

German Vol.5 P.109

Image 4/5.

Ref. SH-RG127

Richard Gutschmidt – The Reigate Squires

Vol.5 Fünf Apfelsinenkerne und andere Detektivgeschichten1902.

REIG: Image 5

German Vol.5 P.122

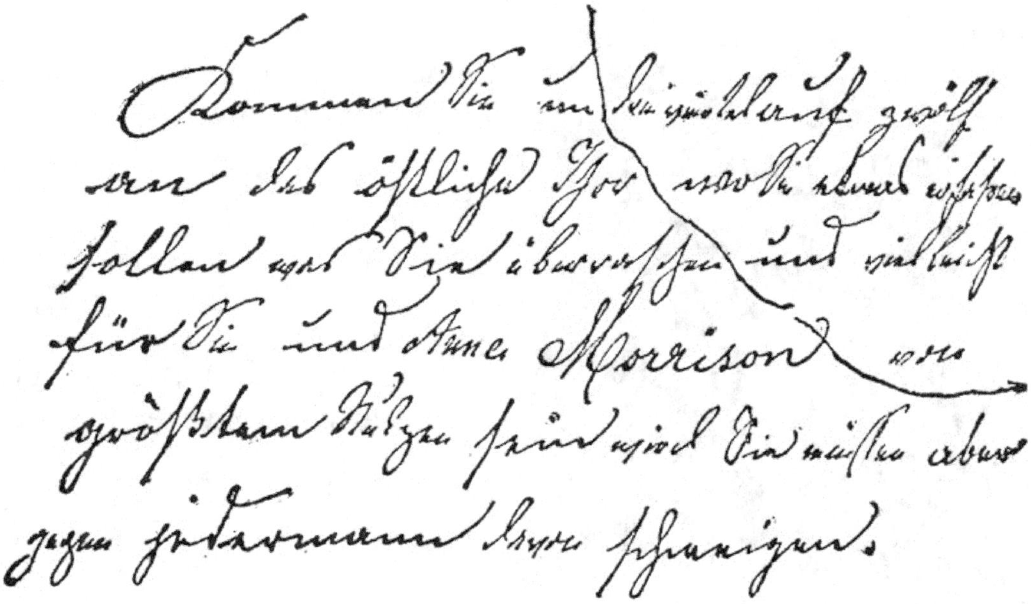

Kommen Sie um drei viertel auf zwölf
an das östliche Thor wo Sie etwas erfahren
sollen was Sie überraschen und vielleicht
für Sie und Anne Morrison von
größtem Nutzen sein wird Sie müssen aber
gegen jedermann darüber schweigen.

Image 5/5.

Ref. SH-RG128

Richard Gutschmidt – The Crooked Man

Vol.5 Fünf Apfelsinenkerne und andere Detektivgeschichten1902.

CROO: Image 1

Sidney Paget.
The Strand, July 1893

SH-SP157. Sidney Paget Original.
"The coachman rushed to the door."

German Vol.5 P.133

Image 1/4.

Ref. SH-RG129

Richard Gutschmidt – The Crooked Man

Vol.5 Fünf Apfelsinenkerne und andere Detektivgeschichten1902.

CROO: Image 2

Sidney Paget.
The Strand, July 1893

SH-SP159. Sidney Paget Original.
"It's Nancy."

German Vol.5 P.145

Image 2/4.

Ref. SH-RG130

Richard Gutschmidt – The Crooked Man

Vol.5 Fünf Apfelsinenkerne und andere Detektivgeschichten1902.

CROO: Image 3

Sidney Paget.
The Strand, July 1893

SH-SP160. Sidney Paget Original. “Mr. Henry Wood, I believe?”

German Vol.5 P.151

Image 3/4.

Ref. SH-RG131

Richard Gutschmidt – The Crooked Man

Vol.5 Fünf Apfelsinenkerne und andere Detektivgeschichten1902.

CROO: Image 4

Sidney Paget.
The Strand, July 1893

SH-SP161. Sidney Paget Original. “I walked right into six of them.”

German Vol.5 P.155

Image 4/4.

Ref. SH-RG132

Richard Gutschmidt – The Resident Patient

Vol.5 Fünf Apfelsinenkerne und andere Detektivgeschichten1902.

RESI: Image 1

Sidney Paget.
The Strand, August 1893

SH-SP164. Sidney Paget Original. "I stared at him in astonishment."

German Vol.5 P.173

Image 1/5.

Ref. SH-RG133

Richard Gutschmidt – The Resident Patient

Vol.5 Fünf Apfelsinenkerne und andere Detektivgeschichten1902.

RESI: Image 2

Sidney Paget.
The Strand, August 1893

SH-SP165. Sidney Paget
Original. “Helped him to a chair.”

German Vol.5 P.178

Image 2/5.

Ref. SH-RG134

Richard Gutschmidt – The Resident Patient

Vol.5 Fünf Apfelsinenkerne und andere Detektivgeschichten1902

RESI: Image 3

Sidney Paget.
The Strand, August 1893

SH-SP166. Sidney Paget Original. “He burst into my consulting room.”

German Vol.5 P.182

Image 3/5.

Ref. SH-RG135

Richard Gutschmidt – The Resident Patient

Vol.5 Fünf Apfelsinenkerne und andere Detektivgeschichten1902

RESI: Image 4

Sidney Paget.
The Strand, August 1893

SH-SP167. Sidney Paget Original. “In his hand he held a pistol.”

German Vol.5 P.186

Image 4/5.

Ref. SH-RG136

Richard Gutschmidt – The Resident Patient

Vol.5 Fünf Apfelsinenkerne und andere Detektivgeschichten1902.

RESI: Image 5

German Vol.5 P.194

Image 5/5.

Ref. SH-RG137

Richard Gutschmidt – The Greek Interpreter

Vol.7 Als Sherlock Holmes aus Lhassa kam sieben Neue Detektivgeschichten 1905.

GREE: Image 1

German Vol.7 P.153

Image 1/3.

Ref. SH-RG138

Richard Gutschmidt – The Greek Interpreter

Vol.7 Als Sherlock Holmes aus Lhassa kam sieben Neue Detektivgeschichten 1905.

GREE: Image 2

German Vol.7 P.159

Image 2/3.

Ref. SH-RG139

Richard Gutschmidt – The Greek Interpreter

Vol.7 Als Sherlock Holmes aus Lhassa kam sieben Neue Detektivgeschichten 1905.

GREE: Image 3
German Vol.7 P.175

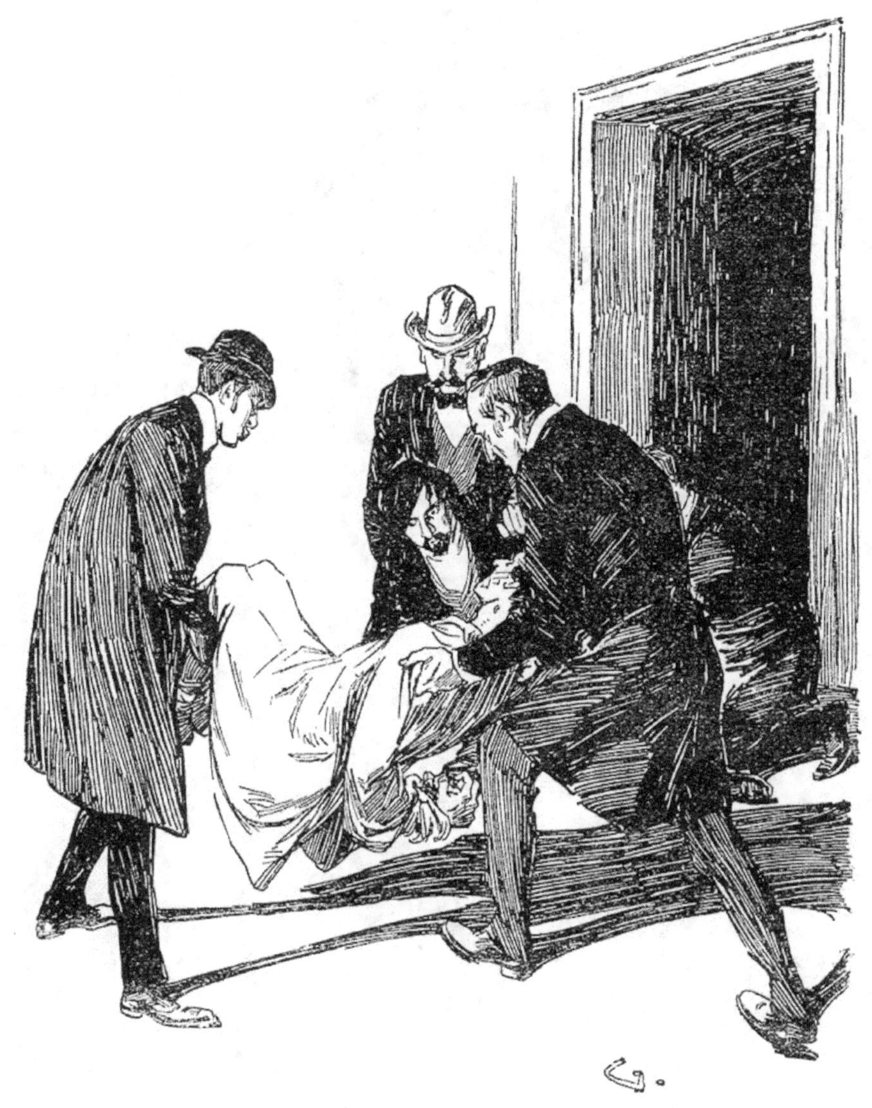

Image 3/3.
Ref. SH-RG140

Richard Gutschmidt – The Naval Treaty

Vol.5 Fünf Apfelsinenkerne und andere Detektivgeschichten1902.

NAVA: Image 1

Sidney Paget.
The Strand, October 1893

SH-SP178. Sidney Paget Original.
"Holmes was working hard over a chemical investigation."

German Vol.5 P.205

Image 1/5.

Ref. SH-RG141

Richard Gutschmidt – The Naval Treaty

Vol.5 Fünf Apfelsinenkerne und andere Detektivgeschichten1902.

German Vol.5 P.210

NAVA: Image 2

Image 2/9.

Ref. SH-RG142

Richard Gutschmidt – The Naval Treaty

Vol.5 Fünf Apfelsinenkerne und andere Detektivgeschichten1902.

German Vol.5 P.215

NAVA: Image 3

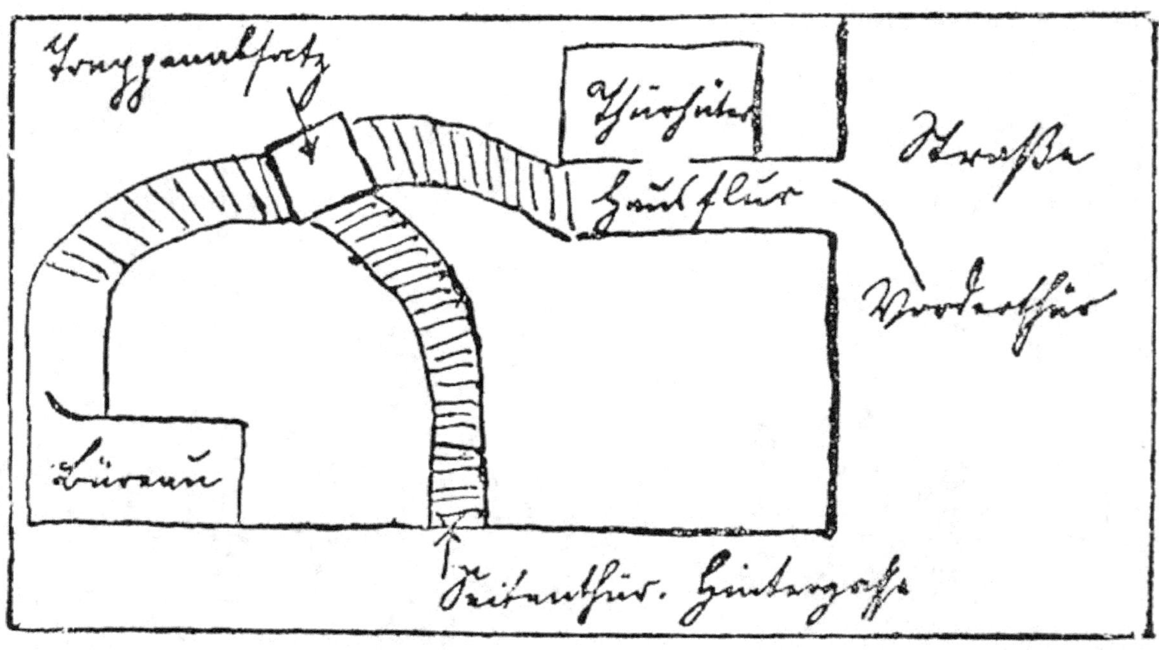

Image 3/9.

Ref. SH-RG143

Richard Gutschmidt – The Naval Treaty

Vol.5 Fünf Apfelsinenkerne und andere Detektivgeschichten1902.

NAVA: Image 4

Sidney Paget.
The Strand,
October 1893

SH-SP182. Sidney Paget Original. “Why, if it isn’t Mr. Phelps!”.”

German Vol.5 P.222

Image 4/9.

Ref. SH-RG144

Richard Gutschmidt – The Naval Treaty

Vol.5 Fünf Apfelsinenkerne und andere Detektivgeschichten1902.

NAVA: Image 5

Sidney Paget.
The Strand,
October 1893

SH-SP184. Sidney Paget Original. "The view was sordid enough."

German Vol.5 P.231

Image 5/9.

Ref. SH-RG145

Richard Gutschmidt – The Naval Treaty

Vol.5 Fünf Apfelsinenkerne und andere Detektivgeschichten1902.

NAVA: Image 6

Sidney Paget.
The Strand, October 1893

SH-SP186. Sidney Paget Original. "A nobleman."

German Vol.5 P.240

Image 6/9.

Ref. SH-RG146

Richard Gutschmidt – The Naval Treaty

Vol.5 Fünf Apfelsinenkerne und andere Detektivgeschichten1902.

NAVA: Image 7

Sidney Paget.
The Strand, September 1893

German Vol.5 P.250

SH-SP188. Sidney Paget Original.
"Holmes examined it critically."

Image 7/9.
Ref. SH-RG147

Richard Gutschmidt – The Naval Treaty

Vol.5 Fünf Apfelsinenkerne und andere Detektivgeschichten1902.

NAVA: Image 8

Sidney Paget.
The Strand, November 1893

SH-SP190. Sidney Paget Original. “Phelps raised the cover.”

German Vol.5 P.261

Image 8/9.

Ref. SH-RG148

Richard Gutschmidt – The Naval Treaty

Vol.5 Fünf Apfelsinenkerne und andere Detektivgeschichten1902.

NAVA: Image 9

Sidney Paget.
The Strand, November 1893

German Vol.5 P.266

SH-SP191. Sidney Paget
Original.
"Joseph Harrison stepped out."

Image 9/9.
Ref. SH-RG149

FINA: Image 1

Sidney Paget.
The Strand, December 1893

German Vol.5 P.280

SH-SP195. Sidney Paget Original.
"Professor Moriarty stood before me."

Image 9/9.
Ref. SH-RG150

FINA: Image 2

Sidney Paget.
The Strand, December 1893

SH-SP197. Sidney Paget Original. "My decrepit Italian friend"

German Vol.5
P.292

Image 2/5.

Ref. SH-RG151

Richard Gutschmidt – The Final Problem

Vol.5 Fünf Apfelsinenkerne und andere Detektivgeschichten1902.

FINA: Image 3

Sidney Paget.
The Strand, December
1893

SH-SP199. Sidney Paget Original. “A large rock clattered down.”

German Vol.5 P.301

Image 3/5.

Ref. SH-RG152

Richard Gutschmidt – The Final Problem

Vol.5 Fünf Apfelsinenkerne und andere Detektivgeschichten1902.

FINA: Image 4

Sidney Paget.
The Strand, December 1893

SH-SP200. Sidney Paget Original. “I saw Holmes gazing down at the rush of the waters.”

German Vol.5 P.305

Image 4/5.

Ref. SH-RG153

Richard Gutschmidt – The Final Problem

Vol.5 Fünf Apfelsinenkerne und andere Detektivgeschichten1902.

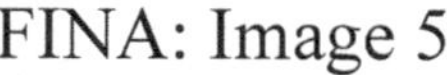

FINA: Image 5

Sidney Paget.
The Strand, December
1893

SH-SP201. Sidney Paget Original. “A small square of paper fluttered down.”

German Vol.5 P.309

Image 5/5.

Ref. SH-RG154

Richard Gutschmidt – The Hound of the Baskervilles

Vol. 6 Der Hund von Baskerville.1905

HOUN: 1

Sidney Paget.
The Strand, April 1901

German Vol.6 P.8

SH-SP203. Sidney Paget Original.
"He looked over it again with a convex lens."

Image 1/30.
Ref. SH-RG155

Richard Gutschmidt – The Hound of the Baskervilles
Vol. 6 Der Hund von Baskerville.1905
HOUN: 2
German Vol.6 P.14

Image 2/30.
Ref. SH-RG156

Richard Gutschmidt – The Hound of the Baskervilles

Vol. 6 Der Hund von Baskerville.1905

HOUN: 3

German Vol.6 P.21

Image 3/30. Page 21.

Ref. SH-RG157

Richard Gutschmidt – The Hound of the Baskervilles

Vol. 6 Der Hund von Baskerville.1905

HOUN: 4

German Vol.6 P.27

Image 4/30.

Ref. SH-RG158

Richard Gutschmidt – The Hound of the Baskervilles
Vol. 6 Der Hund von Baskerville.1905
HOUN: 5
German Vol.6 P.39

Image 5/30.
Ref. SH-RG159

Richard Gutschmidt – The Hound of the Baskervilles

Vol. 6 Der Hund von Baskerville.1905

HOUN: 6

German Vol.6 P.49

Image 6/30.

Ref. SH-RG160

Richard Gutschmidt – The Hound of the Baskervilles
Vol. 6 Der Hund von Baskerville.1905
HOUN: 7
German Vol.6 P.55

Image 7/30.
Ref. SH-RG161

Richard Gutschmidt – The Hound of the Baskervilles

Vol. 6 Der Hund von Baskerville.1905

HOUN: 8

German Vol.6 P.67

Image 8/30.

Ref. SH-RG162

Richard Gutschmidt – The Hound of the Baskervilles

Vol. 6 Der Hund von Baskerville.1905

HOUN: 9

German Vol.6 P.75

Image 9/30.

Ref. SH-RG163

Richard Gutschmidt – The Hound of the Baskervilles
Vol. 6 Der Hund von Baskerville.1905
HOUN: 10
German Vol.6 P.85

Image 10/30.
Ref. SH-RG164

Richard Gutschmidt – The Hound of the Baskervilles

Vol. 6 Der Hund von Baskerville.1905

HOUN: 11

German Vol.6 P.97

Image 11/30.

Ref. SH-RG165

Richard Gutschmidt – The Hound of the Baskervilles
Vol. 6 Der Hund von Baskerville.1905
HOUN: 12
German Vol.6 P.106

Image 12/30.
Ref. SH-RG166

Richard Gutschmidt – The Hound of the Baskervilles

Vol. 6 Der Hund von Baskerville.1905

HOUN: 13

German Vol.6 P.117

Image 13/30.

Ref. SH-RG167

Richard Gutschmidt – The Hound of the Baskervilles
Vol. 6 Der Hund von Baskerville.1905
HOUN: 14
German Vol.6 P.127

Image 14/30.
Ref. SH-RG168

Richard Gutschmidt – The Hound of the Baskervilles
Vol. 6 Der Hund von Baskerville.1905
HOUN: 15
German Vol.6 P.139

Image 15/30.
Ref. SH-RG169

Richard Gutschmidt – The Hound of the Baskervilles
Vol. 6 Der Hund von Baskerville.1905
HOUN: 16
German Vol.6 P.147

Image 16/30.
Ref. SH-RG170

Richard Gutschmidt – The Hound of the Baskervilles

Vol. 6 Der Hund von Baskerville.1905

HOUN: 17

German Vol.6 P.158

Image 17/30.

Ref. SH-RG171

Richard Gutschmidt – The Hound of the Baskervilles
Vol. 6 Der Hund von Baskerville.1905
HOUN: 18
German Vol.6 P.170

Image 18/30.
Ref. SH-RG172

Richard Gutschmidt – The Hound of the Baskervilles

Vol. 6 Der Hund von Baskerville.1905

HOUN: 19

German Vol.6 P.181

Image 19/30.

Ref. SH-RG173

Richard Gutschmidt – The Hound of the Baskervilles

Vol. 6 Der Hund von Baskerville.1905

HOUN: 20

German Vol.6 P.195

Image 20/30.

Ref. SH-RG174

Richard Gutschmidt – The Hound of the Baskervilles

Vol. 6 Der Hund von Baskerville.1905

HOUN: 21

German Vol.6 P.203

Image 21/30.

Ref. SH-RG175

Richard Gutschmidt – The Hound of the Baskervilles
Vol. 6 Der Hund von Baskerville.1905
HOUN: 22
German Vol.6 P.210

Image 22/30.
Ref. SH-RG176

Richard Gutschmidt – The Hound of the Baskervilles

Vol. 6 Der Hund von Baskerville.1905

HOUN: 23

German Vol.6 P.222

Image 23/30.

Ref. SH-RG177

Richard Gutschmidt – The Hound of the Baskervilles

Vol. 6 Der Hund von Baskerville.1905

HOUN: 24

German Vol.6 P.232

Image 24/30.

Ref. SH-RG178

Richard Gutschmidt – The Hound of the Baskervilles
Vol. 6 Der Hund von Baskerville.1905
HOUN: 25
German Vol.6 P.244

Image 25/30.
Ref. SH-RG179

Richard Gutschmidt – The Hound of the Baskervilles
Vol. 6 Der Hund von Baskerville.1905
HOUN: 26
German Vol.6 P.259

Image 26/30.
Ref. SH-RG180

Richard Gutschmidt – The Hound of the Baskervilles

Vol. 6 Der Hund von Baskerville.1905

HOUN: 27

German Vol.6 P.267

Image 27/30.

Ref. SH-RG181

Richard Gutschmidt – The Hound of the Baskervilles

Vol. 6 Der Hund von Baskerville.1905

HOUN: 28

German Vol.6 P.280

Image 28/30.

Ref. SH-RG182

Richard Gutschmidt – The Hound of the Baskervilles

Vol. 6 Der Hund von Baskerville.1905

HOUN: 29

German Vol.6 P.297

Image 29/30.

Ref. SH-RG183

Richard Gutschmidt – The Hound of the Baskervilles
Vol. 6 Der Hund von Baskerville.1905
HOUN: 30
German Vol.6 P.305

Image 30/30.
Ref. SH-RG184

Richard Gutschmidt – The Empty House

Vol. 7 Als Sherlock Holmes aus Lhassa kam sieben Neue Detektivgeschichten1905

EMPT: 1
German Vol.7 P.38

Image 1/3.
Ref. SH-RG185

Richard Gutschmidt – The Empty House

Vol. 7 Als Sherlock Holmes aus Lhassa kam sieben Neue Detektivgeschichten1905

EMPT: 2

German Vol.7 P.22

Image 2/3.

Ref. SH-RG186

Richard Gutschmidt – The Empty House
Vol. 7 Als Sherlock Holmes aus Lhassa kam sieben Neue Detektivgeschichten1905
EMPT: 3
German Vol.7 P.38

Image 3/3.
Ref. SH-RG187

Richard Gutschmidt – The Norwood Builder

Vol. 7 Als Sherlock Holmes aus Lhassa kam sieben Neue Detektivgeschichten1905
NORW: 1
German Vol.7 P.65

Image 1/3.
Ref. SH-RG188

Richard Gutschmidt – The Norwood Builder

Vol. 7 Als Sherlock Holmes aus Lhassa kam sieben Neue Detektivgeschichten1905

NORW: 2

German Vol.7 P.80

Image 2/3.

Ref. SH-RG189

Richard Gutschmidt – The Norwood Builder
Vol. 7 Als Sherlock Holmes aus Lhassa kam sieben Neue Detektivgeschichten1905
NORW: 3
German Vol.7 P.93

Image 3/3.
Ref. SH-RG190

Richard Gutschmidt – The Dancing Men

Vol. 7 Als Sherlock Holmes aus Lhassa kam sieben Neue Detektivgeschichten1905

DANC: 1

German Vol.7 P.22

Image 1/3.

Ref. SH-RG191

Richard Gutschmidt – The Dancing Men
Vol. 7 Als Sherlock Holmes aus Lhassa kam sieben Neue
Detektivgeschichten1905
DANC: 2
German Vol.7 P.35

Image 2/3.
Ref. SH-RG192

Richard Gutschmidt – The Norwood Builder
Vol. 7 Als Sherlock Holmes aus Lhassa kam sieben Neue
Detektivgeschichten1905
DANC: 3
German Vol.7 P.51

Image 3/3.
Ref. SH-RG193

Richard Gutschmidt – The Solitary Cyclist

Vol. 7 Als Sherlock Holmes aus Lhassa kam sieben Neue Detektivgeschichten1905
SOLI: 1
German Vol.7 P.281

Image 1/3.
Ref. SH-RG194

Richard Gutschmidt – The Solitary Cyclist
Vol. 7 Als Sherlock Holmes aus Lhassa kam sieben Neue Detektivgeschichten1905
SOLI: 2
German Vol.7 P.293

Image 2/3.
Ref. SH-RG195

Richard Gutschmidt – The Solitary Cyclist

Vol. 7 Als Sherlock Holmes aus Lhassa kam sieben Neue Detektivgeschichten1905

SOLI: 3

German Vol.7 P.300

Image 3/3.

Ref. SH-RG196

Richard Gutschmidt – The Priory School

Vol. 6 Die tanzenden Männchen und andere Detektivgeschichten 1906
PRIO: 1
German Vol.6 P.75

Image 1/3.
Ref. SH-RG197

Richard Gutschmidt – The Priory School

Vol. 6 Die tanzenden Männchen und andere Detektivgeschichten 1906

PRIO: 2

German Vol.6 P.90

Image 2/3.

Ref. SH-RG198

Richard Gutschmidt – The Priory School

Vol. 6 Die tanzenden Männchen und andere Detektivgeschichten 1906

PRIO: 3

German Vol.6 P.119

Image 3/3.

Ref. SH-RG199

Richard Gutschmidt – Black Peter

Vol. 6 Die tanzenden Männchen und andere Detektivgeschichten 1906
BLAC: 1
German Vol.6 P.126

Image 1/3.
Ref. SH-RG200

Richard Gutschmidt – Black Peter

Vol. 6 Die tanzenden Männchen und andere Detektivgeschichten 1906

BLAC: 2

German Vol.6 P.144

Image 2/3.

Ref. SH-RG201

Richard Gutschmidt – Black Peter

Vol. 6 Die tanzenden Männchen und andere Detektivgeschichten 1906

BLAC: 3

German Vol.6 P.156

Image 3/3.

Ref. SH-RG202

Richard Gutschmidt – Charles Augustus Milverton

Vol. 9 Sherlock Holmes und die Ohren nebst anderen Geschichten 1908

CHAS: 1

German Vol.9

Image 1/5.

Ref. SH-RG203

Richard Gutschmidt – Charles Augustus Milverton

Vol. 9 Sherlock Holmes und die Ohren nebst anderen Geschichten 1908

CHAS: 2

German Vol.9

Image 2/5.

Ref. SH-RG204

Richard Gutschmidt – Charles Augustus Milverton

Vol. 9 Sherlock Holmes und die Ohren nebst anderen Geschichten 1908

CHAS: 3

German Vol.9

Image 3/5.

Ref. SH-RG205

Richard Gutschmidt – Charles Augustus Milverton

Vol. 9 Sherlock Holmes und die Ohren nebst anderen Geschichten 1908

CHAS: 4

German Vol.9

Image 4/5.

Ref. SH-RG206

Richard Gutschmidt – Charles Augustus Milverton

Vol. 9 Sherlock Holmes und die Ohren nebst anderen Geschichten 1908

CHAS: 5

German Vol.9

Image 5/5.

Ref. SH-RG207

Richard Gutschmidt – The Six Napoleons

Vol. 8 Die tanzenden Männchen und andere Detektivgeschichten1906
SIXN: 1
German Vol.8 P.177

Image 1/3.
Ref. SH-RG208

Richard Gutschmidt – The Six Napoleons

Vol. 8 Die tanzenden Männchen und andere Detektivgeschichten1906

SIXN: 2

German Vol.8 P.196

Image 2/3.

Ref. SH-RG209

Richard Gutschmidt – The Six Napoleons
Vol. 8 Die tanzenden Männchen und andere Detektivgeschichten1906
SIXN: 3
German Vol.8 P.203

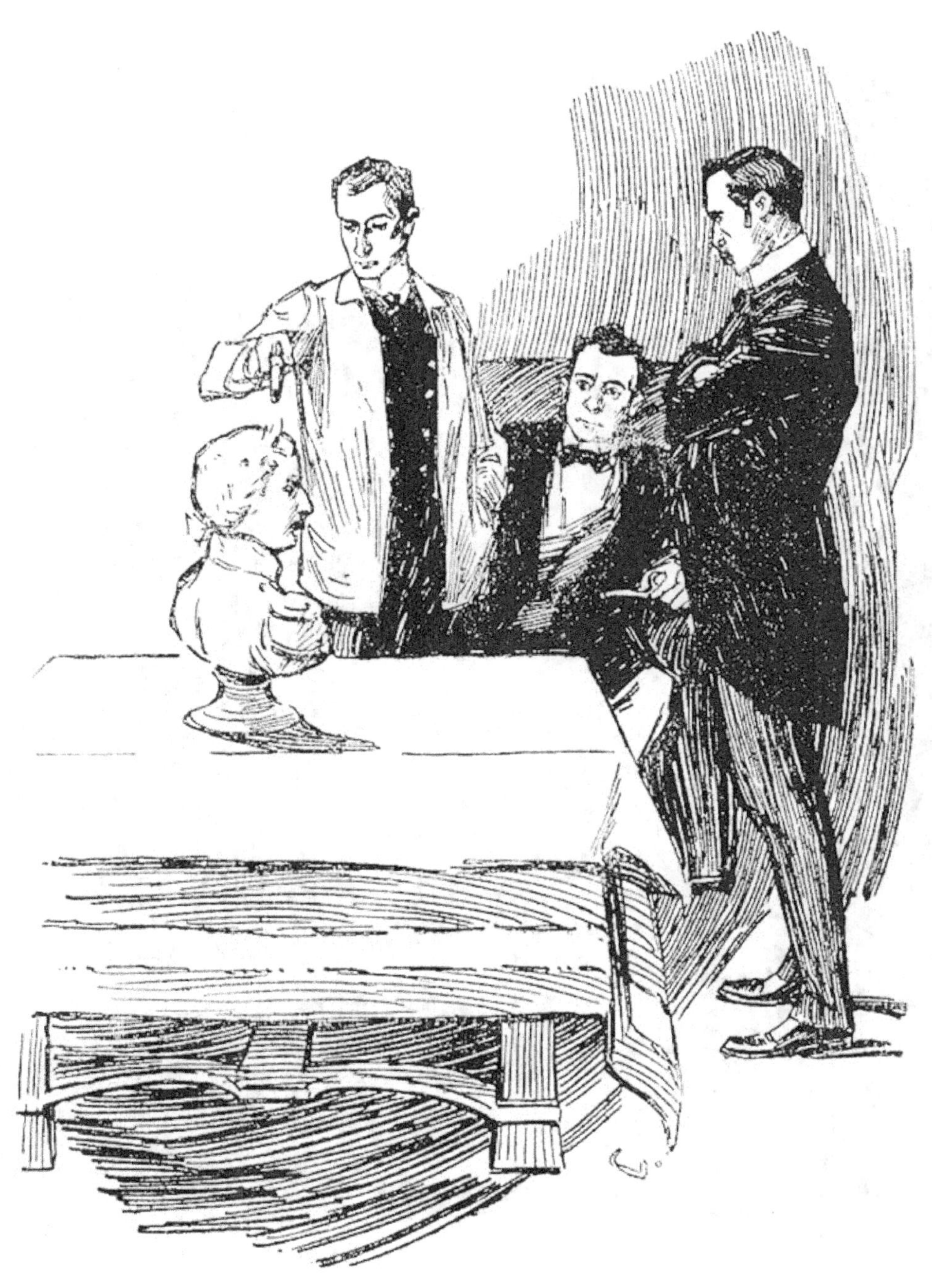

Image 3/3.
Ref. SH-RG210

Richard Gutschmidt – The Three Students

Vol. 9 Sherlock Holmes und die Ohren nebst anderen Geschichten 1908

3STU: 1

German Vol.9

Image 1/4.

Ref. SH-RG211

Richard Gutschmidt – The Three Students

Vol. 9 Sherlock Holmes und die Ohren nebst anderen Geschichten 1908

3STU: 2

German Vol.9

Image 2/4.

Ref. SH-RG212

Richard Gutschmidt – The Three Students

Vol. 9 Sherlock Holmes und die Ohren nebst anderen Geschichten 1908

3STU: 3

German Vol.9

Image 3/4.

Ref. SH-RG213

Richard Gutschmidt – The Three Students

Vol. 9 Sherlock Holmes und die Ohren nebst anderen Geschichten 1908

3STU: 4

German Vol.9

Image 4/4.

Ref. SH-RG214

Richard Gutschmidt – The Gold Pince-Nez

Vol. 7 Als Sherlock Holmes aus Lhassa kam sieben Neue Detektivgeschichten1905
GOLD: 1
German Vol.7 P.233

Image 1/4.
Ref. SH-RG215

Richard Gutschmidt – The Gold Pince-Nez

Vol. 7 Als Sherlock Holmes aus Lhassa kam sieben Neue Detektivgeschichten1905

GOLD: 2

German Vol.7 P.235

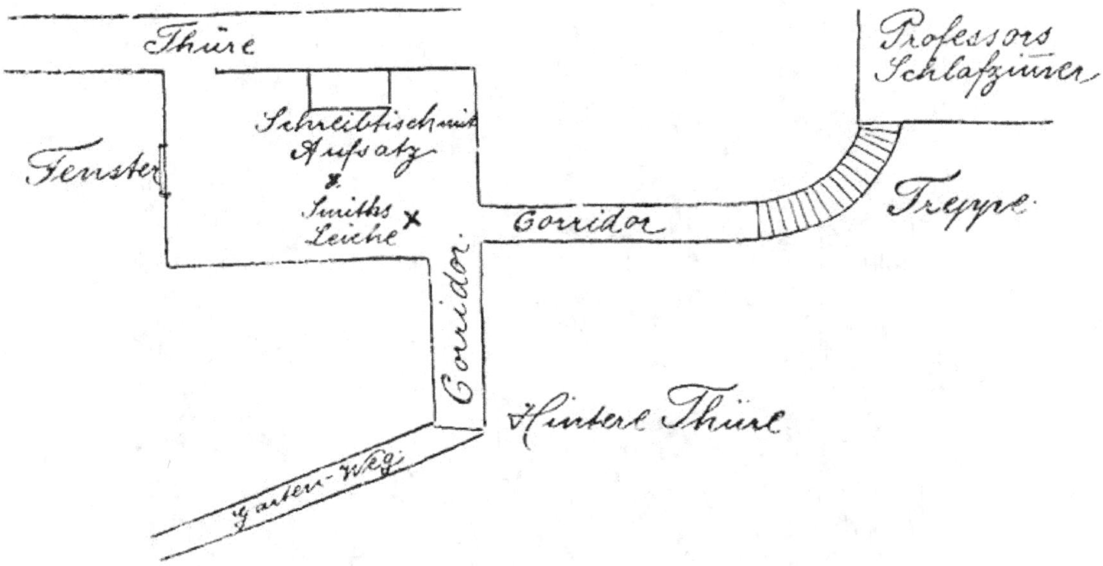

Image 2/4.

Ref. SH-RG216

Richard Gutschmidt – The Gold Pince-Nez
Vol. 7 Als Sherlock Holmes aus Lhassa kam sieben Neue Detektivgeschichten1905
GOLD: 3
German Vol.7 P.250

Image 3/4.
Ref. SH-RG217

Richard Gutschmidt – The Gold Pince-Nez

Vol. 7 Als Sherlock Holmes aus Lhassa kam sieben Neue Detektivgeschichten1905

GOLD: 4

German Vol.7 P.261

Image 4/4.

Ref. SH-RG218

Richard Gutschmidt – The Missing Three-Quarter

Vol. 9 Sherlock Holmes und die Ohren nebst anderen Geschichten 1908
MISS: 1
German Vol.9

Rich. Gutschmidt

Image 1/4.
Ref. SH-RG219

Richard Gutschmidt – The Missing Three-Quarter

Vol. 9 Sherlock Holmes und die Ohren nebst anderen Geschichten 1908

MISS: 2

German Vol.9

Image 2/4.

Ref. SH-RG220

Richard Gutschmidt – The Missing Three-Quarter

Vol. 9 Sherlock Holmes und die Ohren nebst anderen Geschichten 1908

MISS: 3

German Vol.9

Image 3/4.

Ref. SH-RG221

Richard Gutschmidt – The Missing Three-Quarter

Vol. 9 Sherlock Holmes und die Ohren nebst anderen Geschichten 1908

MISS: 4

German Vol.9

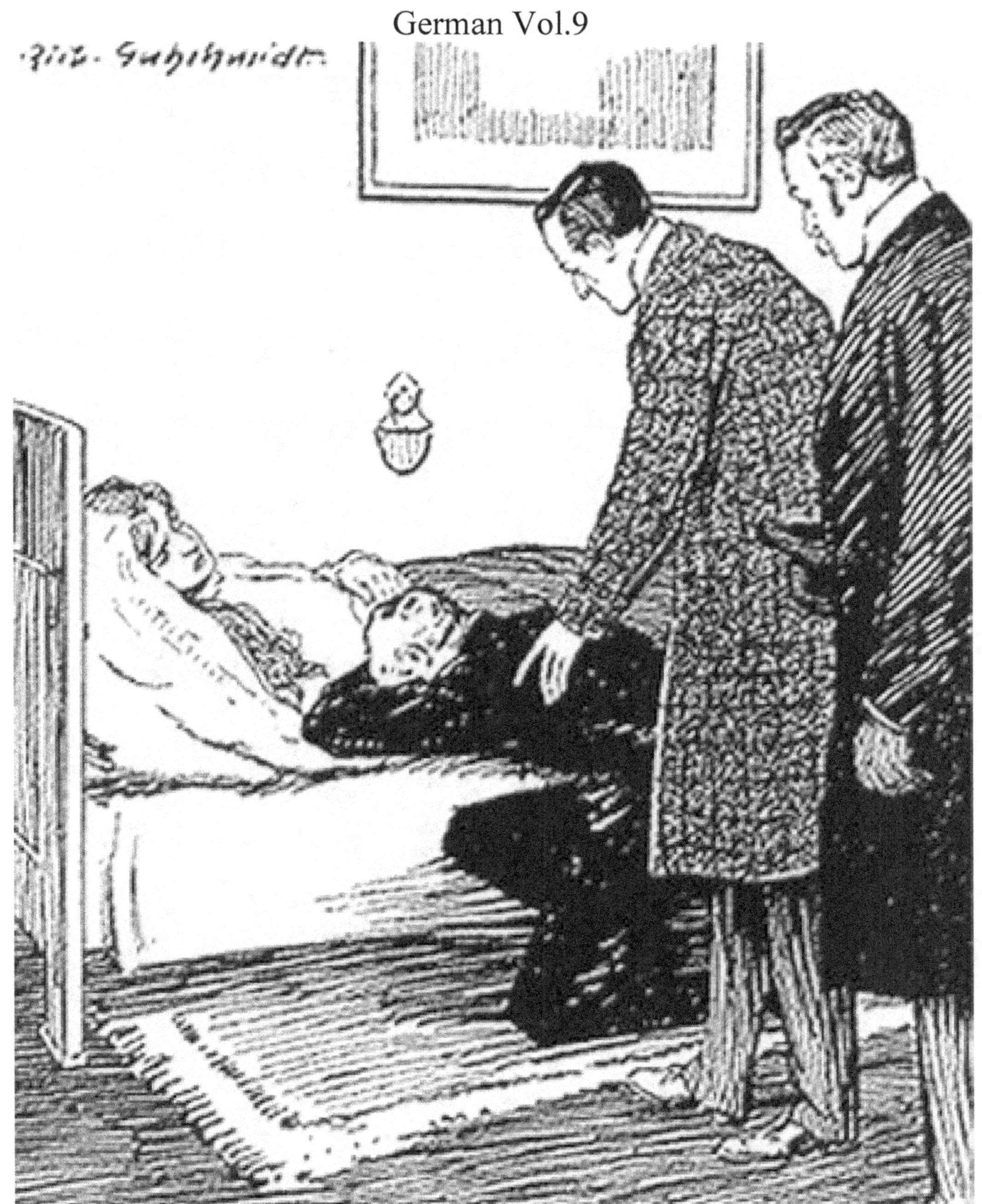

Image 4/4.

Ref. SH-RG222

Richard Gutschmidt – The Abbey Grange

Vol. 8 Die tanzenden Männchen und andere Detektivgeschichten1908
ABBE: 1
German Vol.8 P.217

Image 1/3.
Ref. SH-RG223

Richard Gutschmidt – The Abbey Grange

Vol. 8 Die tanzenden Männchen und andere Detektivgeschichten1908

ABBE: 2

German Vol.8 P.230

Image 2/3.

Ref. SH-RG224

Richard Gutschmidt – The Abbey Grange
Vol. 8 Die tanzenden Männchen und andere Detektivgeschichten1908
ABBE: 3
German Vol.8 P.249

Image 3/3.
Ref. SH-RG225

Richard Gutschmidt – The Second Stain

Vol. 8 Die tanzenden Männchen und andere Detektivgeschichten1908
SECO: 1
German Vol.8 P.269

Image 1/3.
Ref. SH-RG226

Richard Gutschmidt – The Second Stain

Vol. 8 Die tanzenden Männchen und andere Detektivgeschichten1908

SECO: 2

German Vol.8 P.279

Image 2/3.

Ref. SH-RG227

Richard Gutschmidt – The Second Stain

Vol. 8 Die tanzenden Männchen und andere Detektivgeschichten1908

SECO: 3

German Vol.8 P.301

Image 33.

Ref. SH-RG228

Graham Grinham

Very little is known about Graham Grinham apart from the fact he was an American illustrator who did 6 illustrations for Sherlock Holmes Stories between 1911 and 1912 in the St. Louis Star. The St. Louis Star ran from 1884 until 1951. It started out as the St. Louis Sunday Sayings.

A Study in Scarlet	3 illustrations.
The Sign of Four	1 illustrations
A Scandal in Bohemia	1 illustrations
The Red-Headed League	1 illustrations

Graham Grinham – A Study in Scarlet – 12th March 1911 in The St. Louis Star

Page 1. Image 1/3

Graham Grinham – A Study in Scarlet – 12th March 1911 in The St. Louis Star

Page 8. Image 2/3 “How are you?” He said. “You have been in Afghanistan, I perceive.”

Graham Grinham – A Study in Scarlet – 12th March 1911 in The St. Louis Star

Page 9. Image 3/3 "How on Earth did you know that?" I asked in astonishment.

Graham Grinham – A Study in Scarlet – 12th March 1911 in The St. Louis Star

"HOW ARE YOU?" HE SAID. "YOU HAVE BEEN IN AFGHANISTAN, I PERCEIVE."

"HOW ON EARTH DID YOU KNOW THAT?" I ASKED IN ASTONISHMENT.

The images on page 8 & 9 combined to form a complete illustration of Stamford, Watson meeting Holmes in the St. Bart's Laboratory

Graham Grinham – The Sign of the Four – 9th April 1911 in The St. Louis Star

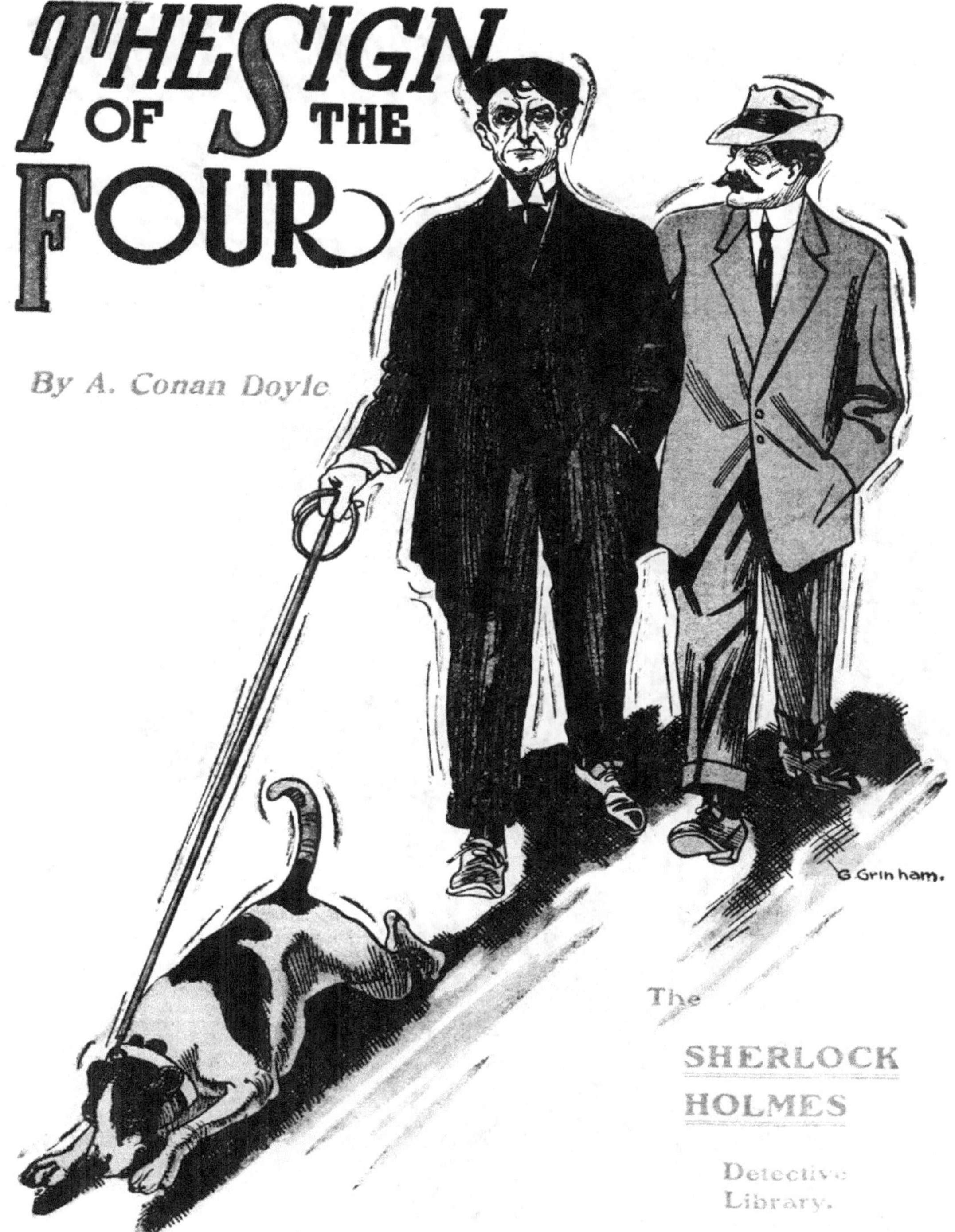

Page 1. Image 1/1

Graham Grinham – A Scandal in Bohemia – 28th May 1911 in The St. Louis Star

Page 1. Image 1/1

Graham Grinham – The Red-Headed League – 8th October 1911 in The St. Louis Star

THE RED-HEADED LEAGUE

A SHERLOCK HOLMES STORY

Page 1. Image 1/1

George Wylie Hutchinson

Born in Great Village, Nova Scotia in 1852.
Died in Clacton-on-Sea, Essex in 1942.

After he left Nova Scotia as a cabin boy at the age of 14, he became a noted painter and illustrator while he lived in Britain.
He produced 42 illustrations for the November 1891 edition of the book A Study in Scarlet by Ward, Lock, Bowden & Co. These images were also used in the 1896 and 1901 editions of this book. Since we know the page numbers of the 1896 edition, these will be the pages quoted.

There is certainly a different style between the Frontispiece and the rest of his illustrations.

George Hutchinson – A Study in Scarlet 1891 and 1896.

Image 1/42. Frontispiece. "Lestrade and Holmes sprang upon him like so many staghounds."
Ref. SH-GH1

George Hutchinson – A Study in Scarlet 1891 and 1896.
The 'IN' in this image is from the start of the Sentence.
IN the year 1878 I took my degree of Doctor of Medicine of the University of London and proceeded to Netley to go through the course prescribed for surgeons in the army.

Image 2/42. Page 1. "There I was struck on the shoulder by a bullet."
Ref. SH-GH2

George Hutchinson – A Study in Scarlet 1891 and 1896.

Image 3/42. Page 9. " 'I've found it! I've found it!' he shouted."
Ref. SH-GH3

George Hutchinson – A Study in Scarlet 1891 and 1896.

The 'WE' in this image is from the start of the Sentence.

WE met next day as he had arranged, and inspected the rooms at No. 221B, Baker Street, of which he had spoken at our meeting.

Image 4/42. Page 16. "He would close his eyes and scrape carelessly at the fiddle."

Ref. SH-GH4.

George Hutchinson – A Study in Scarlet 1891 and 1896.

Image 5/42. Page 23. “There was a little sallow, rat-faced, dark-eyed fellow.”
Ref. SH-GH5

George Hutchinson – A Study in Scarlet 1891 and 1896.

Image 6/42. Page 24. "Grey-Headed, seedy visitor"
Ref. SH-GH6

George Hutchinson – A Study in Scarlet 1891 and 1896.

Image 7/42. Page 26. "An old white-haired gentleman had an interview with my companion." (In some editions these last three illustrations are together on the same page.)
Ref. SH-GH7

George Hutchinson – A Study in Scarlet 1891 and 1896.

The ‘I’ in this image is from the start of the Sentence.
I confess that I was considerably startled by this fresh proof of the practical nature of my companion's theories.

Image 8/42. Page 34. “He hustled on his overcoat.”
Ref. SH-GH8

George Hutchinson – A Study in Scarlet 1891 and 1896.

Image 9/42. Page 44. "Sherlock Holmes approached the body and kneeling down examined it intently."
Ref. SH-GH9

George Hutchinson – A Study in Scarlet 1891 and 1896.

Image 10/42. Page 49. "He struck a match on his boot and held it up against the wall."
Ref. SH-GH10

George Hutchinson – A Study in Scarlet 1891 and 1896.

The 'IT' in this image is from the start of the Sentence.
IT was one o'clock when we left No. 3, Lauriston Gardens.

Image 11/42. Page 54. "He appeared presently, looking a little irritable."
Ref. SH-GH11

George Hutchinson – A Study in Scarlet 1891 and 1896.

Image 12/42. Page 61. "John Rance sprang to his feet with a frightened face."
Ref. SH-GH12

George Hutchinson – A Study in Scarlet 1891 and 1896.

Image 13/42. Page 65. " 'He was an uncommon drunk sort of man.' "
Ref. SH-GH13

George Hutchinson – A Study in Scarlet 1891 and 1896.

The 'OUR' in this image is from the start of the Sentence.
OUR morning's exertions had been too much for my weak health, and I was tired out in the afternoon.

Image 14/42. Page 68. "When I returned with the pistol."
Ref. SH-GH14

Image 15/42. Page 75. “The old crone drew out an evening paper and pointed at our advertisement.”
Ref. SH-GH15

George Hutchinson – A Study in Scarlet 1891 and 1896.

Image 16/42. Page 79. "Her pursuer dogged her some little distance behind."
Ref. SH-GH16

George Hutchinson – A Study in Scarlet 1891 and 1896.

The 'THE' in this image is from the start of the Sentence.

THE papers next day were full of the "Brixton Mystery," as they termed it.

Image 17/42. Page 82. "Came up the stairs three steps at a time."

Ref. SH-GH17

George Hutchinson – A Study in Scarlet 1891 and 1896.

Image 18/42. Page 85. " 'It's the Baker Street division of the Detective Police Force' ."

Ref. SH-GH18

George Hutchinson – A Study in Scarlet 1891 and 1896.

Image 19/42. Page 95. " 'He caught her by the wrist and endeavoured to draw her towards the door.' "
Ref. SH-GH19

George Hutchinson – A Study in Scarlet 1891 and 1896.

The 'THE' in this image is from the start of the Sentence.
THE intelligence with which Lestrade greeted us was so momentous and so unexpected, that we were all three fairly dumfoundered.

Image 20/42. Page 101. " 'He nearly fainted when he saw it.' "
Ref. SH-GH20

George Hutchinson – A Study in Scarlet 1891 and 1896.

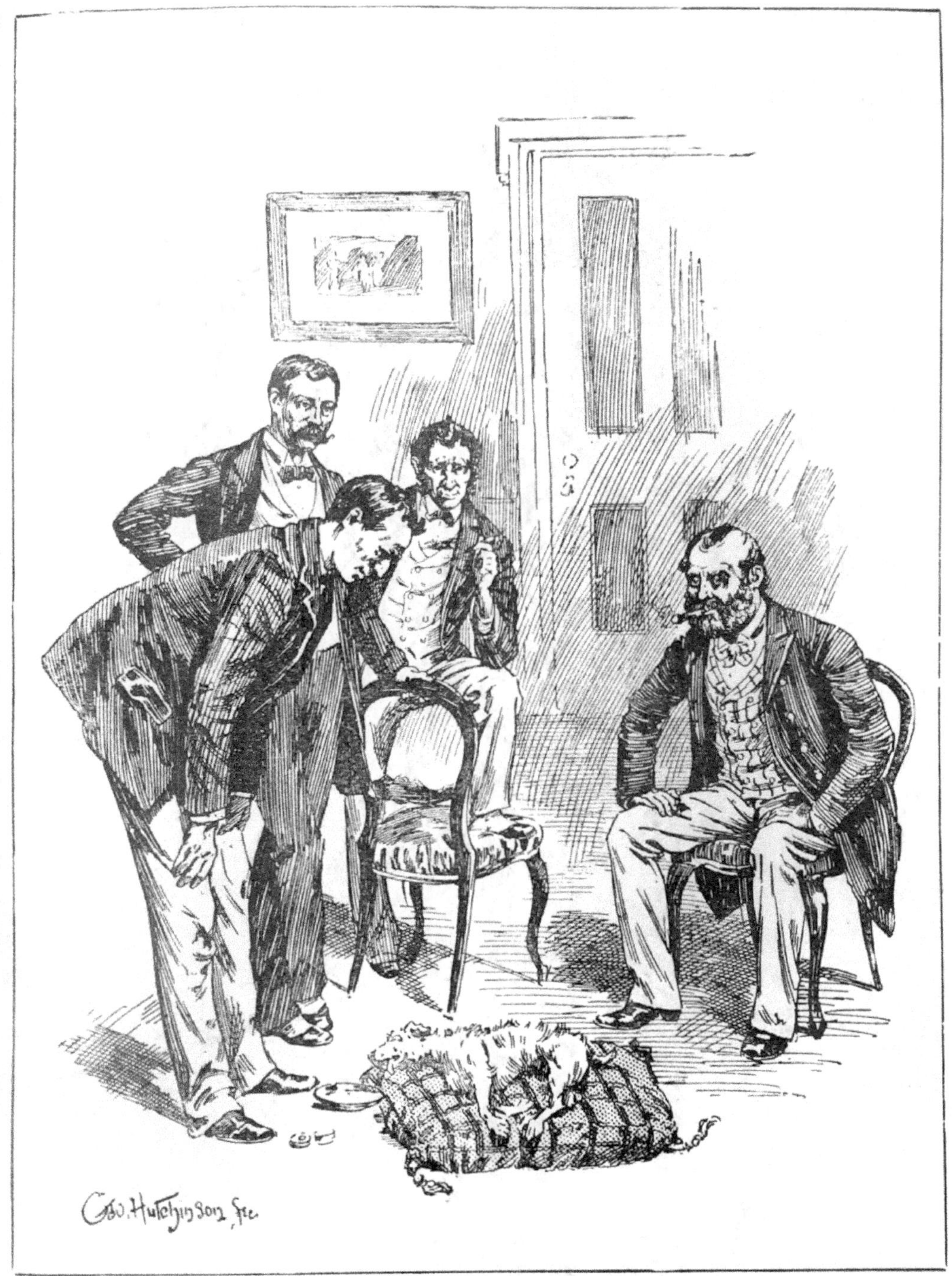

Image 21/42. Page 111. “The unfortunate creature’s tongue seemed hardly to have been moistened in it before it gave a convulsive shiver in every limb and lay as rigid and lifeless as if it had been struck by lightning.”
Ref. SH-GH21

George Hutchinson – A Study in Scarlet 1891 and 1896.

The ‘IN’ in this image is from the start of the Sentence.

IN the central portion of the great North American Continent there lies an arid and repulsive desert, which for many a long year served as a barrier against the advance of civilisation.

Image 22/42. Page 118. “Dying from hunger.”

Ref. SH-GH22

Image 23/42. Page 126. “Side by side on the narrow shawl knelt the two wanderers.”
Ref. SH-GH23

Image 24/42. Page 131. "One of them seized the little girl and hoisted her upon his shoulder."
Ref. SH-GH24

George Hutchinson – A Study in Scarlet 1891 and 1896.

The 'THIS' in this image is from the start of the Sentence.

THIS is not the place to commemorate the trials and privations endured by the immigrant Mormons before they came to their final haven.

Image 25/42. Page 136. "Down the dusty high roads defiled long streams of heavily-laden mules."

Ref. SH-GH25

Image 26/42. Page 142. “A sinewy brown hand caught the frightened horse by the curb.”
Ref. SH-GH26

Image 27/42. Page 146. "One Summer evening he came galloping down the road."
Ref. SH-GH27

George Hutchinson – A Study in Scarlet 1891 and 1896.

The ‘T’ in this image is from the start of the Sentence.

THREE weeks had passed since Jefferson Hope and his comrades had departed from Salt Lake City. John Ferrier's heart was sore within him when he thought of the young man's return, and of the impending loss of his adopted child.

Image 28/42. Page 148. “Armed men, masked, stealthy and noiseless.”
Ref. SH-GH28

George Hutchinson – A Study in Scarlet 1891 and 1896.

Image 29/42. Page 154. “He was passing through the door, when he turned, with flushed face and flashing eyes.”
Ref. SH-GH29

Image 30/42. Page 155. "He was still sitting with his elbow upon his knee."
Ref. SH-GH30

George Hutchinson – A Study in Scarlet 1891 and 1896.

The ‘ON’ in this image is from the start of the Sentence.

ON the morning which followed his interview with the Mormon Prophet, John Ferrier went into Salt Lake City, and having found his acquaintance, who was bound for the Nevada Mountains, he entrusted him with his message to Jefferson Hope.

Image 31/42. Page 79. “A small square of paper pinned on to the coverlet of his bed.”

Ref. SH-GH31

George Hutchinson – A Study in Scarlet 1891 and 1896.

Image 32/42. Page 161. " 'You shall smart for this!' Stangerson cried, white with rage."
Ref. SH-GH32

George Hutchinson – A Study in Scarlet 1891 and 1896.

Image 33/42. Page 167. "He saw to his astonishment a man lying flat upon his face."
Ref. SH-GH33

George Hutchinson – A Study in Scarlet 1891 and 1896.

The ‘ALL in this image is from the start of the Sentence.

ALL night their course lay through intricate defiles and over irregular and rock-strewn paths.

Image 34/42. Page 176. “A great boulder crashed down on him.”
Ref. SH-GH34

Image 35/42. Page 183. “Her pursuer dogged her some little distance behind.”
Ref. SH-GH35

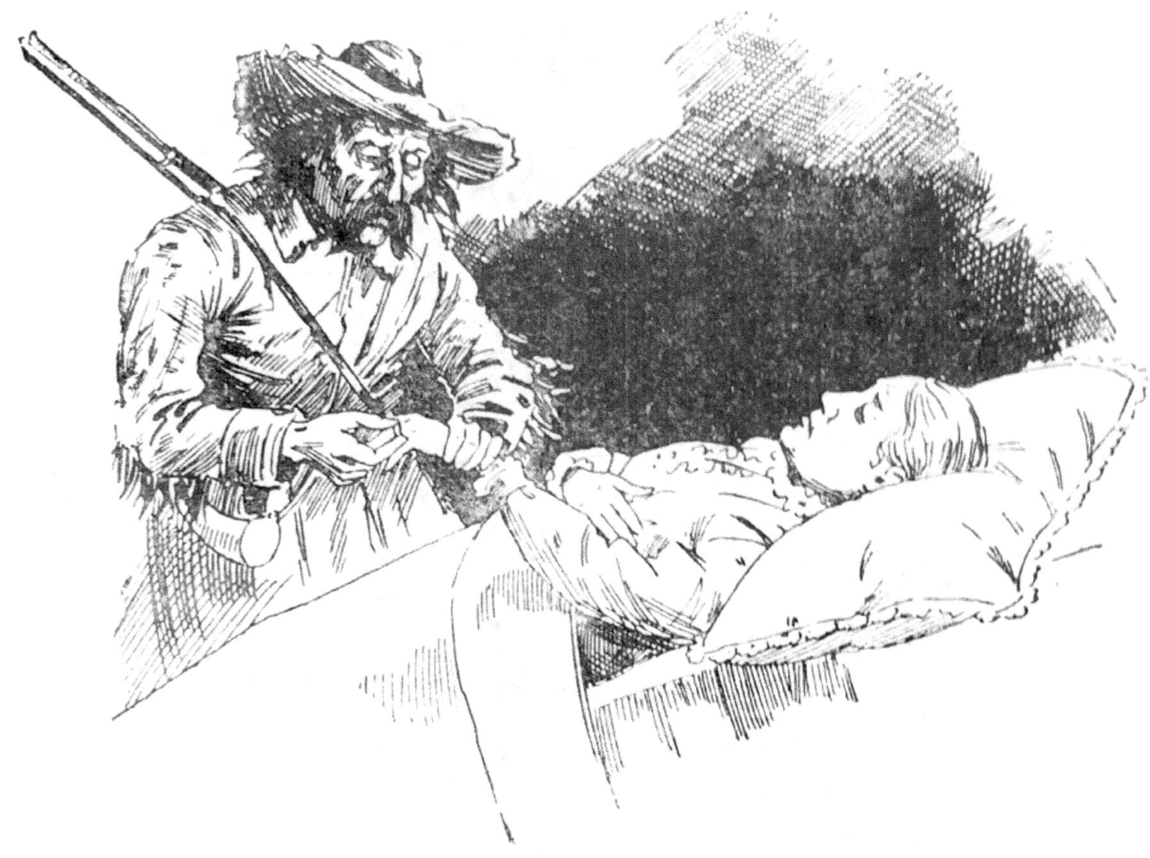

Image 36/42. Page 187. “Snatching up her hand, he took the wedding-ring from her finger.”
Ref. SH-GH36

George Hutchinson – A Study in Scarlet 1891 and 1896.

The 'OUR' in this image is from the start of the Sentence.

OUR prisoner's furious resistance did not apparently indicate any ferocity in his disposition towards ourselves, for on finding himself powerless, he smiled in an affable manner, and expressed his hopes that he had not hurt any of us in the scuffle.

Image 37/42. Page 192. " 'Who am I?' "

Ref. SH-GH37

George Hutchinson – A Study in Scarlet 1891 and 1896.

Image 38/42. Page 207 “He cowered away with wild cries and prayers for mercy.”
Ref. SH-GH38

Image 39/42. Page 210. "He sprang from his bed and flew at my throat."
Ref. SH-GH39

George Hutchinson – A Study in Scarlet 1891 and 1896.

The 'WE' in this image is from the start of the Sentence.

WE had all been warned to appear before the magistrates upon the Thursday; but when the Thursday came there was no occasion for our testimony.

Image 40/42. Page 213. "A higher judge had taken the matter in hand."
Ref. SH-GH40

George Hutchinson – A Study in Scarlet 1891 and 1896.

Image 41/42. Page 221. " 'You may do what you like, Doctor.' "
Ref. SH-GH41

Image 42/42. Page 224.
Ref. SH-GH42

Arthur Twidle

Born in Rotherhithe, Surrey in 1865

Died in Godstone Green, Surrey 25th April 1936

English illustrator and artist, who is best known for his Sherlock Holmes illustrations after the death of Sidney Paget. He also illustrated other Arthur Conan Doyle's works.

He exhibited paintings in oils at the Royal Academy and was well known for his mural, pastels, and panels.

He did an illustration for the frontispiece for the American Publisher D. Appleton & Co's for their 1906 edition of the Study in scarlet

Wisteria Lodge 10 illustrations

In the December 1908 edition of The Strand Magazine, 6 of his illustrations were used for The Bruce-Parting Plans story.

Arthur Twidle – A Study in Scarlet 1903 (Published by D. Appleton & Co.)

Frontispiece image

Ref. SH-AT1

Arthur Twidle – The Adventure of Wisteria Lodge (The Strand Magazine, September 1908.)

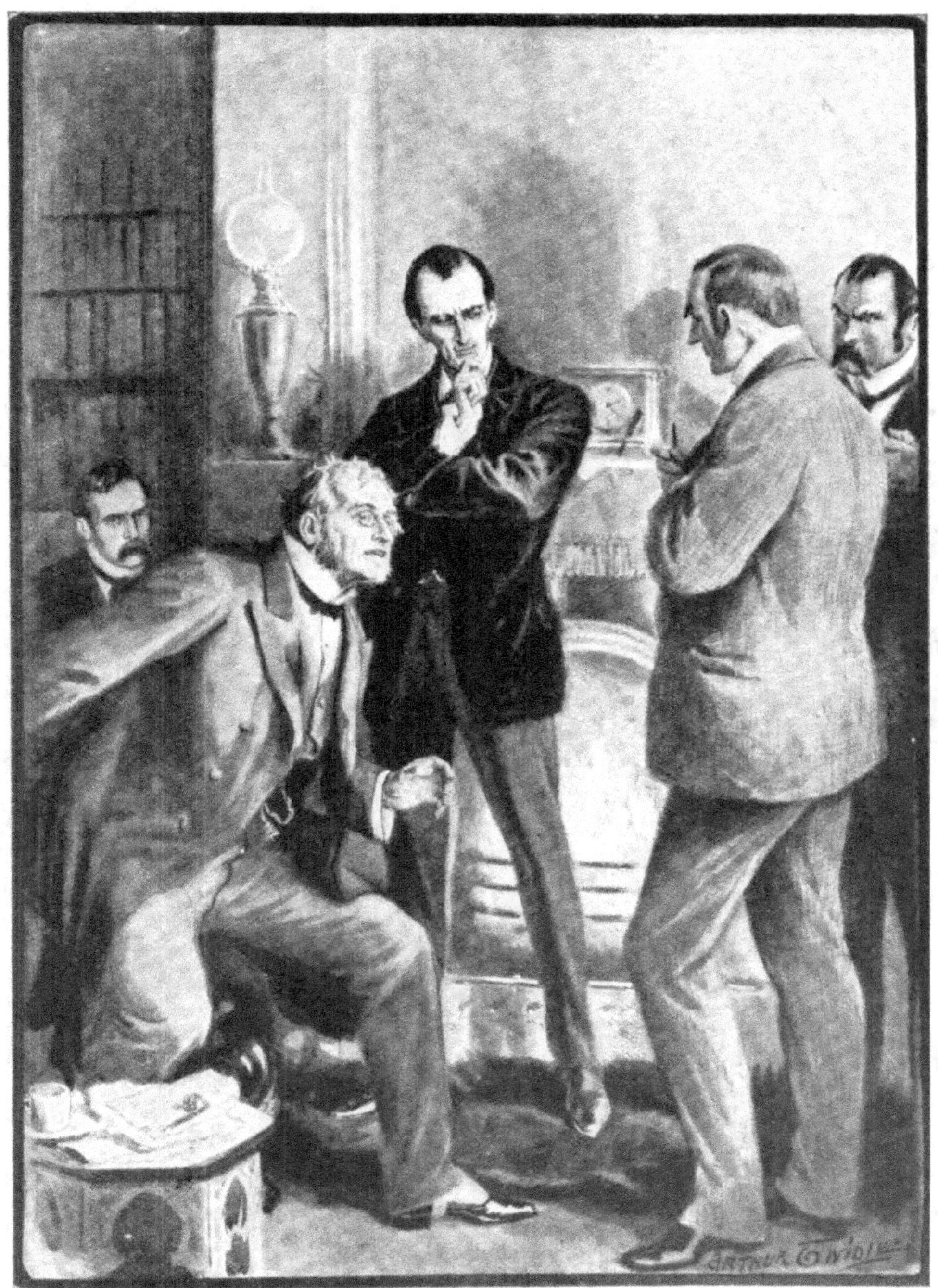

Image 1/10 Page 242. This is awful! You don't mean – You don't mean that I am suspected? *(See page 245)*[2]

Ref. SH-AT2

[2] This is reference to the Strand Magazine page, not this book.

Arthur Twidle – The Adventure of Wisteria Lodge (The Strand Magazine, September 1908.)

Image 2/10 Page 244. But I have been running around and making inquiries before I came to you.

Ref. SH-AT3

Arthur Twidle – The Adventure of Wisteria Lodge (The Strand Magazine, September 1908.)

Image 3/10 Page 247. "It was a dog-grate, Mr. Holmes, and he overpitched it, I picked this out unburned from the back of it."

Ref. SH-AT4

Arthur Twidle – The Adventure of Wisteria Lodge (The Strand Magazine, September 1908.)

Image 4/10 Page 250. "He tossed it across with a laugh."
Ref. SH-AT5

Arthur Twidle – The Adventure of Wisteria Lodge (The Strand Magazine, October 1908.)

Image 5/10 Page 362. " 'Very interesting indeed,' said Holmes."

(See page 364.)

Ref. SH-AT6

Arthur Twidle – The Adventure of Wisteria Lodge (The Strand Magazine, October 1908.)

Image 6/10 Page 364. "There was a face looking in at me through the lower pane."

Ref. SH-AT7

Arthur Twidle – The Adventure of Wisteria Lodge (The Strand Magazine, October 1908.)

Image 7/10 Page 365. "He drew a zinc pail from under the sink." *Ref. SH-AT8.*

Arthur Twidle – The Adventure of Wisteria Lodge (The Strand Magazine, October 1908.)

Image 8/10 Page 367. "The man walked into the trap and was captured."
Ref. SH-AT9

Arthur Twidle – The Adventure of Wisteria Lodge (The Strand Magazine, October 1908.)

Image 9/10 Page 370. “She fought her way out again.”
Ref. SH-AT10

Arthur Twidle – The Adventure of Wisteria Lodge (The Strand Magazine, October 1908.)

Image 10/10 Page 372. "He and his master dragged me to my room."
Ref. SH-AT11

Arthur Twidle – The Adventure of the Bruce-Partington Plans (The Strand Magazine, December 1908.)

Image 1/6 Page 691. “The tall and portly form of Mycroft Holmes was ushered into the room.”

Ref. SH-AT12

Arthur Twidle – The Adventure of the Bruce-Partington Plans (The Strand Magazine, December 1908.)

Image 2/6 Page 694. "My friend was standing with an expression of strained intensity upon his face."

Ref. SH-AT13

Arthur Twidle – The Adventure of the Bruce-Partington Plans (The Strand Magazine, December 1908.)

Image 3/6 Page 698. "Do you mean to say that anyone holding these three papers, and without the seven others, could construct a Bruce-Partington Submarine?"

Ref. SH-AT14

Arthur Twidle – The Adventure of the Bruce-Partington Plans (The Strand Magazine, December 1908.)

Image 4/6 Page 701. "Halloa, Watson! What is this?"

Ref. SH-AT15

Arthur Twidle – The Adventure of the Bruce-Partington Plans (The Strand Magazine, December 1908.)

Image 5/6 Page 703. "Before our prisoner had recovered his balance the door was shut and Holmes standing with his back against it."

Ref. SH-AT16

Arthur Twidle – The Adventure of the Bruce-Partington Plans (The Strand Magazine, December 1908.)

Image 6/6 Page 705. "That was the end of the matter."

Ref. SH-AT17

Thomas Jeffs Nicholl

Born ; Dublin, Ireland in 1851
Died : Tacoma, Washington in 1931.
Known for his Landscape and coastal subjects and 33 illustrations for the Sherlock Holmes Story The Sign of (the) Four, that were serialized over 14 weeks in the Wilson Advance publication.

Week	Date	Illustrations
1	7th Mar 1895	5
2	14th Mar 1895	3
3	21st Mar 1895	2
4	28th Mar 1895	3
5	4th Apr 1895	3
6	11th Apr 1895	2
7	18th Apr 1895	2
8	25th Apr 1895	2
9	2nd May 1895	2
10	16th May 1895	2
11	23rd May 1895	2
12	30th May 1895	1
13	6th Jun 1895	3
14	13th Jun 1895	1

Thomas Jeffs Nicholl – The Sign of the Four (The Wilson Advance, 7th March – 13th June 1895.)

7th March 1895. Image 1/33. The Sign of the Four

Ref. SH-TJN1

Thomas Jeffs Nicholl – The Sign of the Four (The Wilson Advance, 7th March – 13th June 1895.)
The 'S' in this image is from the start of the Sentence.
Sherlock Holmes took his bottle from the corner of the mantel-piece, and his hypodermic syringe from its neat morocco case.

7th March 1895. Image 2/33. Dropped Capital 'S'
Ref. SH-TJN2

Thomas Jeffs Nicholl – The Sign of the Four (The Wilson Advance, 7th March – 13th June 1895.)

7th March 1895. Image 3/33. "My mind rebels at stagnation."
Ref. SH-TJN3

Thomas Jeffs Nicholl – The Sign of the Four (The Wilson Advance, 7th March – 13th June 1895.)

7th March 1895. Image 4/33. He balanced the watch in his hand.

Ref. SH-TJN4

Thomas Jeffs Nicholl – The Sign of the Four (The Wilson Advance, 7th March – 13th June 1895.)

7th March 1895. Image 5/33. "You will, I am sure, excuse me."
Ref. SH-TJN5

Thomas Jeffs Nicholl – The Sign of the Four (The Wilson Advance, 7th March – 13th June 1895.)

14th March 1895. Image 6/33. "I sat in the window, volume in hand." *Ref. SH-TJN6*

Thomas Jeffs Nicholl – The Sign of the Four (The Wilson Advance, 7th March – 13th June 1895.)

14th March 1895. Image 7/33. "The Sahib aw(a)its you."

Ref. SH-TJN7

Thomas Jeffs Nicholl – The Sign of the Four (The Wilson Advance, 7th March – 13th June 1895.)

14th March 1895. Image 8/33. “That would hardly do.” He cried.”
Ref. SH-TJN8

Thomas Jeffs Nicholl – The Sign of the Four (The Wilson Advance, 7th March – 13th June 1895.)

21st March 1895. Image 9/33. "The little man stopped to light his Hookah." *Ref. SH-TJN9*

Thomas Jeffs Nicholl – The Sign of the Four (The Wilson Advance, 7th March – 13th June 1895.)

21st March 1895. Image 10/33. "He held up the lantern."

Ref. SH-TJN10

Thomas Jeffs Nicholl – The Sign of the Four (The Wilson Advance, 7th March – 13th June 1895.)

28th March 1895. Image 11/33. "He was stiff and cold."

Ref. SH-TJN11

Thomas Jeffs Nicholl – The Sign of the Four (The Wilson Advance, 7th March – 13th June 1895.)

28th March 1895. Image 12/33. "He held down the lamp to the floor."
Ref. SH-TJN12

Thomas Jeffs Nicholl – The Sign of the Four (The Wilson Advance, 7th March – 13th June 1895.)

28th March 1895. Image 13/33. "Confirms it in every respect."

Ref. SH-TJN13

Thomas Jeffs Nicholl – The Sign of the Four (The Wilson Advance, 7th March – 13th June 1895.)

4th April 1895. Image 14/33. "Now stand clear."

Ref. SH-TJN14

Thomas Jeffs Nicholl – The Sign of the Four (The Wilson Advance, 7th March – 13th June 1895.)

4th April 1895. Image 15/33. "With a light spring he came on the barrel."
Ref. SH-TJN15

Thomas Jeffs Nicholl – The Sign of the Four (The Wilson Advance, 7th March – 13th June 1895.)

4th April 1895. Image 16/33. "Holmes clambered up and took the dog from me."

Ref. SH-TJN16

Thomas Jeffs Nicholl – The Sign of the Four (The Wilson Advance, 7th March – 13th June 1895.)

11th April 1895. Image 17/33. "Toby stood upon the case."

Ref. SH-TJN17

Thomas Jeffs Nicholl – The Sign of the Four (The Wilson Advance, 7th March – 13th June 1895.)

11th April 1895. Image 18/33. "I'm sorry, Mrs. Smith, for I wanted a steam launch."

Ref. SH-TJN18

Thomas Jeffs Nicholl – The Sign of the Four (The Wilson Advance, 7th March – 13th June 1895.)

18th April 1895. Image 19/33. "A Guinea to the boy that finds the boat."
Ref. SH-TJN19

Thomas Jeffs Nicholl – The Sign of the Four (The Wilson Advance, 7th March – 13th June 1895.)

18th April 1895. Image 20/33. "Clad in rude sailor dress."

Ref. SH-TJN20

Thomas Jeffs Nicholl – The Sign of the Four (The Wilson Advance, 7th March – 13th June 1895.)

25th April 1895. Image 21/33. "What is it, my man? I asked.

Ref. SH-TJN21

Thomas Jeffs Nicholl – The Sign of the Four (The Wilson Advance, 7th March – 13th June 1895.)

25th April 1895. Image 22/33. Jones, Holmes and I sat on the deck.
Ref. SH-TJN22

Thomas Jeffs Nicholl – The Sign of the Four (The Wilson Advance, 7th March – 13th June 1895.)

2nd May 1895. Image 23/33. "And there is the Aurora! Exclaimed Holmes.
Ref. SH-TJN23

Thomas Jeffs Nicholl – The Sign of the Four (The Wilson Advance, 7th March – 13th June 1895.)

2nd May 1895. Image 24/33. He shook his two clinched fist at us.
Ref. SH-TJN24

Thomas Jeffs Nicholl – The Sign of the Four (The Wilson Advance, 7th March – 13th June 1895.)

16th May 1895. Image 25/33. "Quite a family party," he remarked
Ref. SH-TJN25

Thomas Jeffs Nicholl – The Sign of the Four (The Wilson Advance, 7th March – 13th June 1895.)

16th May 1895. Image 26/33. "The Treasure is lost," said Miss Morstan. *Ref. SH-TJN26*

Thomas Jeffs Nicholl – The Sign of the Four (The Wilson Advance, 7th March – 13th June 1895.)

23rd May 1895. Image 27/33. How he lost his leg.

Ref. SH-TJN27

Thomas Jeffs Nicholl – The Sign of the Four (The Wilson Advance, 7th March – 13th June 1895.)

23rd May 1895. Image 28/33. I used to stand outside the gateway.
Ref. SH-TJN28

Thomas Jeffs Nicholl – The Sign of the Four (The Wilson Advance, 7th March – 13th June 1895.)

30th May 1895. Image 29/33."What have you in the bundle?" (I) asked. *Ref. SH-TJN29*

Thomas Jeffs Nicholl – The Sign of the Four (The Wilson Advance, 7th March – 13th June 1895.)

6th June 1895. Image 30/33."I wish to have your advice, Major."

Ref. SH-TJN30

Thomas Jeffs Nicholl – The Sign of the Four (The Wilson Advance, 7th March – 13th June 1895.)

6th June 1895. Image 31/33. I struck him full.

Ref. SH-TJN31

Thomas Jeffs Nicholl – The Sign of the Four (The Wilson Advance, 7th March – 13th June 1895.)

6th June 1895. Image 32/33. We were picked up by a Trader.

Ref. SH-TJN32

Thomas Jeffs Nicholl – The Sign of the Four (The Wilson Advance, 7th March – 13th June 1895.)

13th June 1895. Image 33/33.The End.

Ref. SH-TJN33

Raymond Pallier

Born 1888
Died unknown.
French Cartoonist who did 108 illustrations for the Sherlock Holmes story The Hound of the Baskervilles. Hound was serialised over 19 weeks in Le Petit Journal illustré from 23rd Oct 1921 until 26th Feb 1922.

No.	Date	Parts
1	23/10/1921	8
2	30/10/1921	7
3	6/11/1921	7
4	13/11/1921	4
5	20/11/1921	5
6	27/11/1921	5
7	4/12/1921	5
8	11/12/1921	5
9	18/12/1921	5
10	25/12/1921	5
11	1/1/1922	6
12	8/1/1922	6
13	15/1/1922	6
14	22/1/1922	5
15	29/1/1922	5
16	5/2/1922	6
17	12/2/1922	5
18	19/2/1922	6
19	26/2/1922	7

Raymond Pallier – The Hound of the Baskervilles (1/19). 23rd Oct 1921

Images 1/8. Page 511. Title Page
SH-RP1.

Raymond Pallier – The Hound of the Baskervilles (1/19). 23rd Oct 1921

Images 2/8. Page 511. Sherlock Holmes relaxes in a chair at 221b Baker Street.
SH-RP2.

Raymond Pallier – The Hound of the Baskervilles (1/19). 23rd Oct 1921

Images 3/8. Page 511. An unknown Doctor has left his walking cane, Holmes deduces various aspects of the physician's character from a walking stick the former had left behind.
SH-RP3.

Raymond Pallier – The Hound of the Baskervilles (1/19). 23rd Oct 1921

Images 4/8. Page 511. Doctor Mortimer returns and talks to Holmes about the curse of the Baskervilles and the imminent arrival of the new heir, Sir Henry Baskerville.
SH-RP4.

Raymond Pallier – The Hound of the Baskervilles (1/19). 23rd Oct 1921

Images 5/8. Page 511. Doctor Mortimer Reaches into his pocket to bring out an ancient document dating back to 1742, that tells how Hugo Baskerville had brought a curse upon the Baskerville family in the shape of a spectral giant hound. He then over the next few images tells his tale
SH-RP5.

Raymond Pallier – The Hound of the Baskervilles (1/19). 23rd Oct 1921

Images 6/8. Page 512. "The Manor of Baskerville, Dartmoor in the time of Hugo Baskerville (Cir. 1640s), a most wild, profane, and godless man." *SH-RP6.*

Raymond Pallier – The Hound of the Baskervilles (1/19). 23rd Oct 1921

Images 7/8. Page 512. “t chanced that this Hugo came to love (if, indeed, so dark a passion may be known under so bright a name) the daughter of a yeoman who held lands near the Baskerville estate. But the young maiden, being, discreet and of good repute, would ever avoid him, for she feared his evil name. So it came to pass that one Michaelmas this Hugo, with five or six of his idle and wicked companions, stole down upon the farm and carried off the maiden”
SH-RP7.

Raymond Pallier – The Hound of the Baskervilles (1/19). 23rd Oct 1921

Images 8/8. Page 512. "The young maiden manages to escape and Whereat Hugo ran from the house, crying to his grooms that they should saddle his mare and unkennel the pack, and giving the hounds a kerchief of the maid's, he swung them to the line, and so off full cry in the moonlight over the moor." *SH-RP8.*

Raymond Pallier – The Hound of the Baskervilles (2/19). 30th Oct 1921

Images 1/7. Page 523. "Standing over Hugo, and plucking at his throat, there stood a foul thing, a great, black beast, shaped like a hound, yet larger than any hound that ever mortal eye has rested upon. And even as they looked the thing tore the throat out of Hugo Baskerville."
SH-RP9.

Raymond Pallier – The Hound of the Baskervilles (2/19). 30th Oct 1921

Images 2/7. Page 523. "Sir Charles Baskerville was in the habit every night before going to bed of walking down the famous Yew Alley of Baskerville Hall."
SH-RP10.

Raymond Pallier – The Hound of the Baskervilles (2/19). 30th Oct 1921

Images 3/7. Page 523. "One fact which has not been explained is the statement of Barrymore that his master's footprints altered their character from the time he passed the moor-gate, and that he appeared from thence onwards to have been walking upon his toes."
SH-RP11.

Raymond Pallier – The Hound of the Baskervilles (2/19). 30th Oct 1921

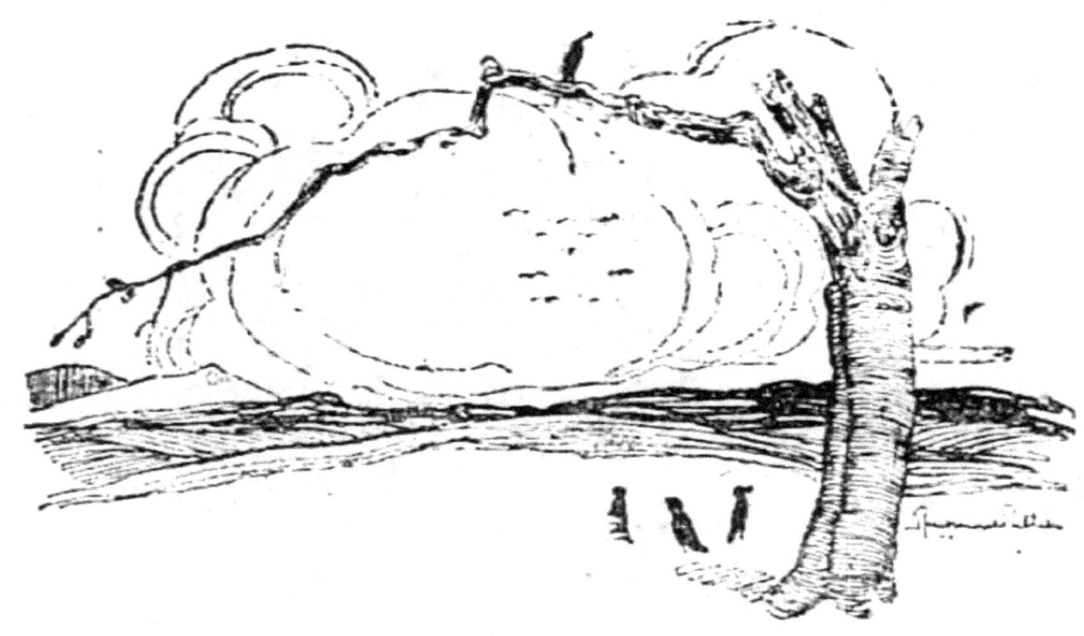

Images 4/7. Page 523. "On the night of Sir Charles's death Barrymore, the butler, who made the discovery, sent Perkins the groom on horseback to me, and as I was sitting up late, I was able to reach Baskerville Hall within an hour of the event."
SH-RP12.

Raymond Pallier – The Hound of the Baskervilles (2/19). 30th Oct 1921

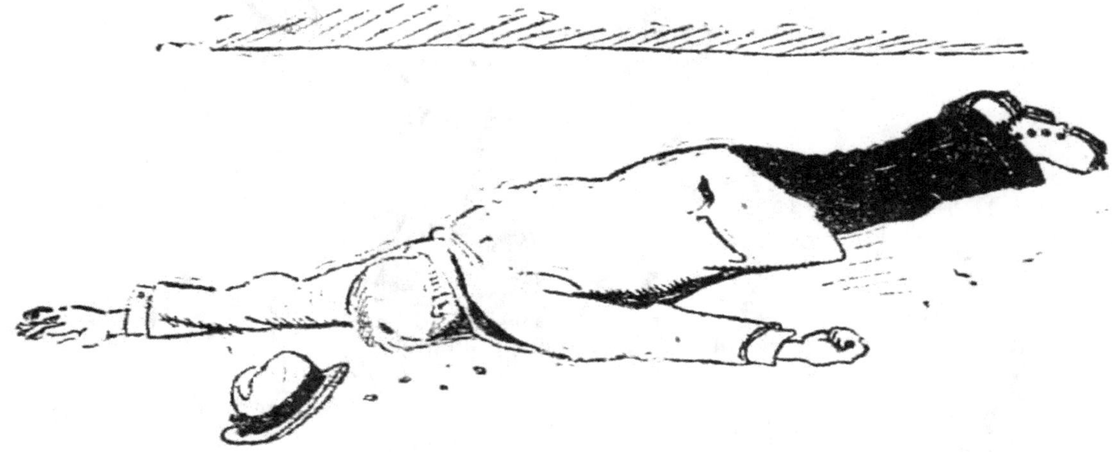

Images 5/7. Page 523. "I carefully examined the body, which had not been touched until my arrival. Sir Charles lay on his face, his arms out, his fingers dug into the ground, and his features convulsed with some strong emotion to such an extent that I could hardly have sworn to his identity."
SH-RP13.

Raymond Pallier – The Hound of the Baskervilles (2/19). 30th Oct 1921

Images 6/7. Page 523. "I find that before the terrible event occurred several people had seen a creature upon the moor which corresponds with this Baskerville demon, and which could not possibly be any animal known to science. They all agreed that it was a huge creature, luminous, ghastly, and spectral. I have cross-examined these men, one of them a hardheaded countryman, one a farrier, and one a moorland farmer."
SH-RP14.

Raymond Pallier – The Hound of the Baskervilles (2/19). 30th Oct 1921

Images 7/7. Page 523. Dr. Mortimer wanted to be advised by Holmes as to what he should do with Sir Henry Baskerville, who would be arriving at Waterloo Station shortly. He was the heir to the Baskerville Estate. *SH-RP15.*

Raymond Pallier – The Hound of the Baskervilles (3/19). 6th Nov 1921

Images 1/7. Page 535. Grimpen, Dartmoor.
SH-RP16.

Raymond Pallier – The Hound of the Baskervilles (3/19). 6th Nov 1921

Images 2/7. Page 535. Now however Sir Henry Baskerville had arrived in England.
SH-RP17.

Raymond Pallier – The Hound of the Baskervilles (3/19). 6th Nov 1921

Images 3/7. Page 535. Sir Henry Baskerville had received a warning letter, he shows it to Holmes. Across the middle of it a single sentence had been formed by the expedient of pasting printed words upon it. It ran: 'as you value your life or your reason keep away from the moor.' The word 'moor' only was printed in ink.
SH-RP18.

Raymond Pallier – The Hound of the Baskervilles (3/19). 6th Nov 1921

Images 4/7. Page 535. Dr. Mortimer is impressed with Holmes' deductions regarding the mysterious letter.
SH-RP19.

Raymond Pallier – The Hound of the Baskervilles (3/19). 6th Nov 1921

Images 5/7. Page 536. Sir Henry Baskerville and Dr. Mortimer leave Baker Street and head back to their hotel.
SH-RP20.

Raymond Pallier – The Hound of the Baskervilles (3/19). 6th Nov 1921

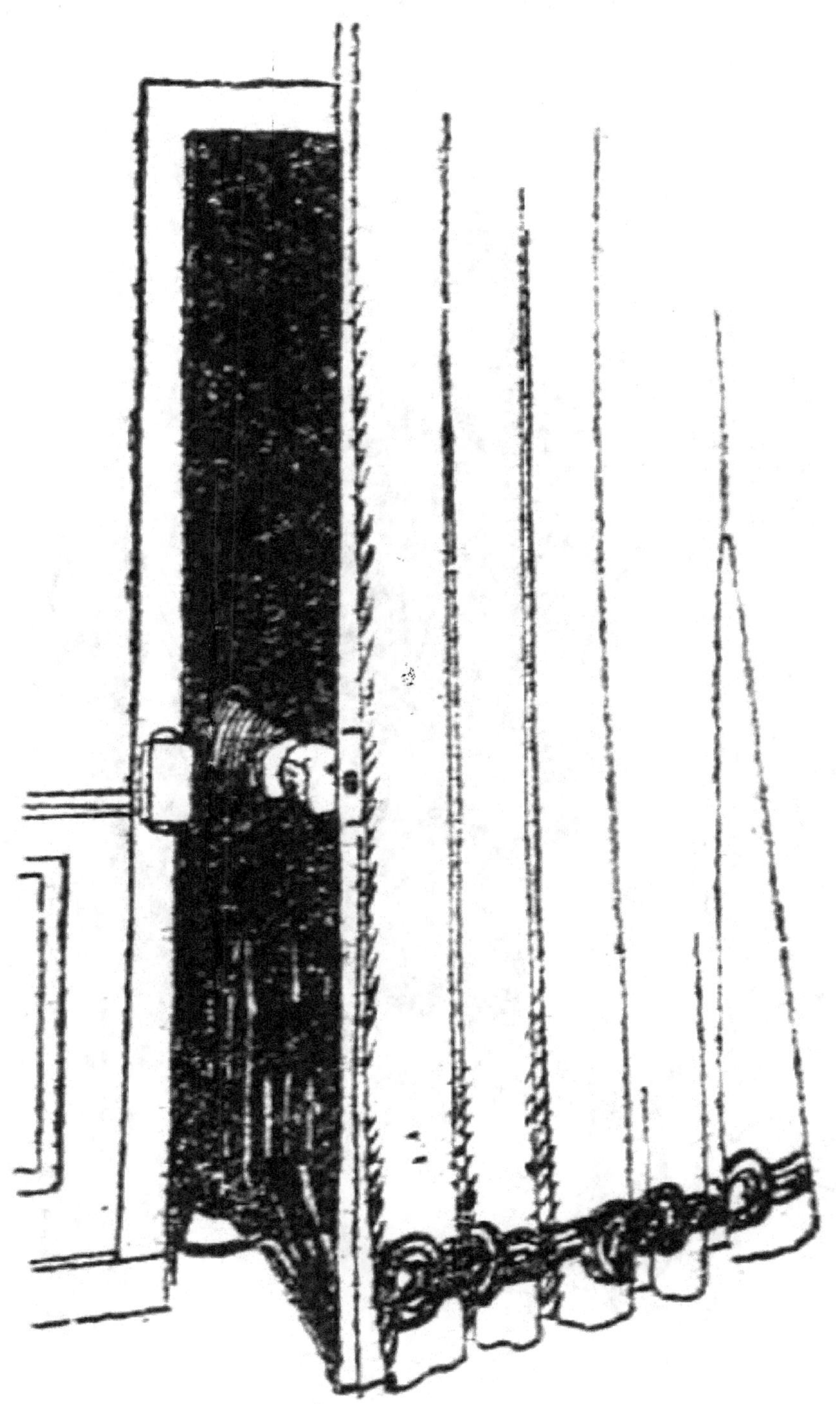

Images 6/7. Page 536. Someone had stolen Sir Henry Baskervilles' boots. (twice)
SH-RP21.

Raymond Pallier – The Hound of the Baskervilles (3/19). 6th Nov 1921

Images 7/7. Page 536. There is a Hansom cab following Sir Henry and Dr. Mortimer while they walk the streets of London.
SH-RP22.

Raymond Pallier – The Hound of the Baskervilles (4/19). 13th Nov 1921

Images 1/4. Page 547 Cartwright. - A lad of fourteen, with a bright, keen face, had obeyed the summons of the manager. He stood now gazing with great reverence at the famous detective.
SH-RP23.

Raymond Pallier – The Hound of the Baskervilles (4/19). 13th Nov 1921

Images 2/4. Page 547. Holmes and Watson ask about any people who had checked into the Northumberland Hotel after Sir Henry Baskerville.
SH-RP24.

Raymond Pallier – The Hound of the Baskervilles (4/19). 13th Nov 1921

Images 3/4. Page 548. The boot boy fails to find out what has happened to Sir Henry's missing shoes.
SH-RP25.

Raymond Pallier – The Hound of the Baskervilles (4/19). 13th Nov 1921

Images 4/4. Page 548 Holmes wants to find out if it was John Barrymore who was trailing Sir Henry, so he has a telegraph sent to him at Baskerville Hall, but the mailman delivers it to his wife Eliza Barrymore.
SH-RP26.

Raymond Pallier – The Hound of the Baskervilles (5/19). 20th Nov 1921

Images 1/5. Page 559.Dr. Watson agrees to accompany Sir Henry Baskerville down to his ancestral home on Dartmoor.
SH-RP27.

Raymond Pallier – The Hound of the Baskervilles (5/19). 20th Nov 1921

Images 2/5. Page 559. Sir Henry Baskerville finds one boot, but another one has gone missing.
SH-RP28.

Raymond Pallier – The Hound of the Baskervilles (5/19). 20th Nov 1921

Images 3/5. Page 559. The man who drove the cab that followed Sir Henry and Dr. Mortimer through London is interviewed by Holmes and says that his passenger was the famous detective Sherlock Holmes.
SH-RP29.

Raymond Pallier – The Hound of the Baskervilles (5/19). 20th Nov 1921

Images 4/5. Page 559. On the journey to the station, Holmes gives instructions to Watson regarding his trip down to Baskerville Hall.
SH-RP30.

Raymond Pallier – The Hound of the Baskervilles (5/19). 20th Nov 1921

Images 5/5. Page 560. Dr. Mortimer and Sir Henry await Dr. Watson's arrival at the train station.
SH-RP31.

Raymond Pallier – The Hound of the Baskervilles (6/19). 27th Nov 1921

Images 1/5. Page 571. Sir Henry on the train going down to Dartmoor, clearly it was not a non-smoker.
SH-RP32.

Raymond Pallier – The Hound of the Baskervilles (6/19). 27th Nov 1921

Images 2/5. Page 571. The porter and others prepare to unload Sir Henry's luggage.
SH-RP33.

Raymond Pallier – The Hound of the Baskervilles (6/19). 27th Nov 1921

Images 3/5. Page 571. John Barrymore the butler is ready to receive the new lord.
SH-RP34.

Raymond Pallier – The Hound of the Baskervilles (6/19). 27th Nov 1921

Images 4/5. Page 572. Dr. Watson is woken up in the night by the sound of a woman sobbing.
SH-RP35.

Raymond Pallier – The Hound of the Baskervilles (6/19). 27th Nov 1921

Images 5/5. Page 572. Watson asks Sir Henry 'Did you, for example, happen to hear someone, a woman I think, sobbing in the night?' to which the answer is 'That is curious, for I did when I was half asleep fancy that I heard something of the sort.'
SH-RP36.

Raymond Pallier – The Hound of the Baskervilles (7/19). 4th Dec 1921

Images 1/5. Page 583. John Barrymore denied that it was his wife who had been sobbing, but he lied, and her tell-tale eyes were red and glanced at Watson from between swollen lids. It was she, then, who wept in the night, *SH-RP37.*

Raymond Pallier – The Hound of the Baskervilles (7/19). 4th Dec 1921

Images 2/5. Page 583. Jack Stapleton. - He was a small, slim, clean-shaven, prim-faced man, flaxen-haired and lean-jawed, between thirty and forty years of age, dressed in a grey suit and wearing a straw hat. A tin box for botanical specimens hung over his shoulder, and he carried a green butterfly-net in one of his hands
SH-RP38.

Raymond Pallier – The Hound of the Baskervilles (7/19). 4th Dec 1921

Images 3/5. Page 583. Cartwright is now down on Dartmoor acting as a messenger/delivery boy to a mysterious person camped out on the moor. *SH-RP39.*

Raymond Pallier – The Hound of the Baskervilles (7/19). 4th Dec 1921

Images 4/5. Page 584. Dr. Watson meets up with Stapleton on the moors and discuss the great Grimpen Mire and how dangerous it is, 'A false step yonder means death to man or beast.' Which nicely sets up the next illustrations *SH-RP40.*

Raymond Pallier – The Hound of the Baskervilles (7/19). 4th Dec 1921

Images 5/5. Page 584. Stapleton says 'Only yesterday I saw one of the moor ponies wander into it. He never came out. I saw his head for quite a long time craning out of the bog-hole, but it sucked him down at last.'
SH-RP41.

Raymond Pallier – The Hound of the Baskervilles (8/19). 11th Dec 1921

Images 1/5. Page 595. Beryl Stapleton. - Slim, elegant, and tall. She had a proud, finely cut face, so regular that it might have seemed impassive were it not for the sensitive mouth and the beautiful dark, eager eyes
SH-RP42.

Raymond Pallier – The Hound of the Baskervilles (8/19). 11th Dec 1921

Images 2/5. Page 595. Miss Stapleton mistakes Dr. Watson for Sir Henry and tries to warm him about the peril of continuing to live at Baskerville Hall. *SH-RP43.*

Raymond Pallier – The Hound of the Baskervilles (8/19). 11th Dec 1921

Images 3/5. Page 595. Stapleton runs off chasing a Cyclopides butterfly in the direction of Grimpen Mire, with the knowledge that he can safely travel through that deadly area.
SH-RP44.

Raymond Pallier – The Hound of the Baskervilles (8/19). 11th Dec 1921

Images 4/5. Page 596. Stapleton took Sir Henry and Dr. Watson to show them the spot where the legend of the wicked Hugo was supposed to have had its origin.
SH-RP45.

Raymond Pallier – The Hound of the Baskervilles (8/19). 11th Dec 1921

Images 5/5. Page 596. Sir Henry meets with Jack Stapleton at Merripit house. He also makes the acquaintance with Beryl Stapleton and is strongly attracted to her.
SH-RP46.

Raymond Pallier – The Hound of the Baskervilles (9/19). 18th Dec 1921

Images 1/5. Page 607. Dr Mortimer lunched with Sir Henry and Watson. He has been excavating a barrow at Long Down and has got a prehistoric skull which fills him with great joy. Never was there such a single-minded enthusiast as he!
SH-RP47.

Raymond Pallier – The Hound of the Baskervilles (9/19). 18th Dec 1921

Images 2/5. Page 607. Mr. Frankland of Lafter Hall, a keen astronomer with a passion for British Law and litigation. Father of estranged Laura Lyons. *SH-RP48.*

Raymond Pallier – The Hound of the Baskervilles (9/19). 18th Dec 1921

Images 3/5. Page 607. John Barrymore creeps around at night, but he is not going to be caught just yet.
SH-RP49.

Raymond Pallier – The Hound of the Baskervilles (9/19). 18th Dec 1921

Images 4/5. Page 608. Dr. Mortimer visits.
SH-RP50.

Raymond Pallier – The Hound of the Baskervilles (9/19). 18th Dec 1921

Images 5/5. Page 608. Sir Henry Baskerville sneaks out to have a rendezvous with Beryl Stapleton without Dr. Watson.
SH-RP51.

Raymond Pallier – The Hound of the Baskervilles (10/19). 25th Dec 1921

Images 1/5. Page 627.Dr. Watson follows Sir Henry Baskerville as he has a clandestine meeting with Beryl Stapleton.
SH-RP52.

Raymond Pallier – The Hound of the Baskervilles (10/19). 25th Dec 1921

Images 2/5. Page 627. Our friend, Sir Henry, and the lady had halted on the path and were standing deeply absorbed in their conversation, when I was suddenly aware that I was not the only witness of their interview.
SH-RP53.

Raymond Pallier – The Hound of the Baskervilles (10/19). 25th Dec 1921

Images 3/5. Page 627. The naturalist's angry gestures showed that the lady was included in his displeasure. it seems that he did not like his sister meeting with Sir Henry Baskerville.
SH-RP54.

Raymond Pallier – The Hound of the Baskervilles (10/19). 25th Dec 1921

Images 4/5. Page 628. Dr. Watson sat up with Sir Henry in his room until nearly three o'clock in the morning, but no sound of any sort did they hear except the chiming clock upon the stairs. The next night they heard someone creeping by outside their room.
SH-RP55.

Raymond Pallier – The Hound of the Baskervilles (10/19). 25th Dec 1921

Images 5/5. Page 628. John Barrymore was waving a candle at a window, clearly signalling to someone. But he is caught by Dr. Watson and Sir Henry. *SH-RP56.*

Raymond Pallier – The Hound of the Baskervilles (11/19). 1st Jan 1922

Images 1/6. Page 7.John Barrymore refuses to explain his actions until Eliza his wife turns up and explains that the convict on the moor is actually her little brother and they have been leaving food and clothing out for him.
SH-RP57.

Raymond Pallier – The Hound of the Baskervilles (11/19). 1st Jan 1922

Images 2/6. Page 7.Sir Henry and Dr. Watson venture out to try and capture the convict Selden on the moor.

SH-RP58.

Raymond Pallier – The Hound of the Baskervilles (11/19). 1st Jan 1922

Images 3/6. Page 7. Selden the convict is waiting for food because of the signal light from John Barrymore. He didn't know that two others were out to try and capture him.
SH-RP59.

Raymond Pallier – The Hound of the Baskervilles (11/19). 1st Jan 1922

Images 4/6. Page 7. Sir Henry and Dr. Watson try and get closer to the convict Selden,
SH-RP60.

Raymond Pallier – The Hound of the Baskervilles (11/19). 1st Jan 1922

Images 5/6. Page 8. Sir Henry and Dr. Watson fail to capture the convict and rest before heading back the Baskerville Hall.
SH-RP61.

Raymond Pallier – The Hound of the Baskervilles (11/19). 1st Jan 1922

Images 6/6. Page 8. Watson continues to write his daily journal for Holmes. *SH-RP62.*

Raymond Pallier – The Hound of the Baskervilles (12/19). 8th Jan 1922

Images 1/6. Page 19. Sir Henry Baskerville.
SH-RP63.

Raymond Pallier – The Hound of the Baskervilles (12/19). 8th Jan 1922

Images 2/6. Page 19. Dr. Watson talks to Sir Henry Baskerville.

Raymond Pallier – The Hound of the Baskervilles (12/19). 8th Jan 1922

Images 3/6. Page 19. Barrymore relates more info. 'Well, Sir Henry, your uncle had a letter that morning. He had usually a great many letters, for he was a public man and well known for his kind heart, so that everyone who was in trouble was glad to turn to him. But that morning, as it chanced, there was only this one letter, so I took the more notice of it. It was from Coombe Tracey, and it was addressed in a woman's hand.'
'Well?'
'Well, sir, I thought no more of the matter, and never would have done had it not been for my wife. Only a few weeks ago she was cleaning out Sir Charles's study - it had never been touched since his death - and she found the ashes of a burned letter in the back of the grate. The greater part of it was charred to pieces, but one little slip, the end of a page, hung together, and the writing could still be read, though it was grey on a black ground. It seemed to us to be a postscript at the end of the letter, and it said: "Please, please, as you are a gentleman, burn this letter, and be at the gate by ten o'clock." Beneath it were signed the initials L.L.'
SH-RP65.

Raymond Pallier – The Hound of the Baskervilles (12/19). 8th Jan 1922

Images 4/6. Page 20. The information from John Barrymore is most useful.
SH-RP66.

Raymond Pallier – The Hound of the Baskervilles (12/19). 8th Jan 1922

Images 5/6. Page 20. October 17th - All day to-day the rain poured down, rustling on the ivy and dripping from the eaves. I thought of the convict out upon the bleak, cold, shelter-less moor. Poor fellow! Whatever his crimes, he has suffered something to atone for them.
SH-RP67.

Raymond Pallier – The Hound of the Baskervilles (12/19). 8th Jan 1922

Images 6/6. Page 20. Dr. Mortimer gives Dr. Watson a ride in this carriage.
SH-RP68.

Raymond Pallier – The Hound of the Baskervilles (13/19). 15th Jan 1922

Images 1/6. Page 31. Cartwright is on his way to meet up with the stranger, unaware that his progress has been observed by old Frankland.
SH-RP69.

Raymond Pallier – The Hound of the Baskervilles (13/19). 15th Jan 1922

Images 2/6. Page 31. Dr. Mortimer plays cards with Sir Henry Baskerville.
SH-RP70.

Raymond Pallier – The Hound of the Baskervilles (13/19). 15th Jan 1922

Images 3/6. Page 31. When Dr. Watson arrives at Laura Lyon's home, he is greeted by her maid.
SH-RP71.

Raymond Pallier – The Hound of the Baskervilles (13/19). 15th Jan 1922

Images 4/6. Page 31. Laura Lyons, daughter of Frankland.
SH-RP72.

Raymond Pallier – The Hound of the Baskervilles (13/19). 15th Jan 1922

Images 5/6. Page 32. Laura Lyons with her husband.
SH-R73.

Raymond Pallier – The Hound of the Baskervilles (13/19). 15th Jan 1922

Images 6/6. Page 32. Dr. Watson doesn't get any information out of Laura Lyons.
SH-RP74.

Raymond Pallier – The Hound of the Baskervilles (14/19). 22nd Jan 1922

Images 1/5. Page 43. Frankland greets Dr. Watson.
SH-RP75.

Raymond Pallier – The Hound of the Baskervilles (14/19). 22nd Jan 1922

Images 2/5. Page 43. Frankland says he knows where the convict is because he says he had been watching a boy take out supplies to him.
SH-RP76.

Raymond Pallier – The Hound of the Baskervilles (14/19). 22nd Jan 1922

Images 3/5. Page 43. This image and the next image are actually the wrong way around. Dr. Watson finds that someone is living in this hut. This is clearly inside the hut, but the next image is him outside.
SH-RP77.

Raymond Pallier – The Hound of the Baskervilles (14/19). 22nd Jan 1922

Images 4/5. Page 44. Dr. Watson braves himself before entering the hut to see who is living inside.
SH-RP78.

Raymond Pallier – The Hound of the Baskervilles (14/19). 22nd Jan 1922

Images 5/5. Page 44. *Baskerville Hall.*
SH-RP79.

Raymond Pallier – The Hound of the Baskervilles (15/19). 29th Jan 1922

Images 1/5. Page 55. The locals are upset with Frankland., he says "I act entirely from a sense of public duty. I have no doubt, for example, that the Fernworthy people will burn me in effigy to-night. I told the police last time they did it that they should stop these disgraceful exhibitions."
SH-RP80.

Raymond Pallier – The Hound of the Baskervilles (15/19). 29th Jan 1922

Images 2/5. Page 55. Sherlock Holmes and Cartwright.
SH-RP81.

Raymond Pallier – The Hound of the Baskervilles (15/19). 29th Jan 1922

Images 3/5. Page 55. Dr. Watson searching the moors. I don't know why this image was used because Dr. Watson's actions are covered in image 14/19) on 22nd Jan 1922
SH-RP82.

Raymond Pallier – The Hound of the Baskervilles (15/19). 29th Jan 1922

Images 4/5. Page 56. Laura Lyons and Jack Stapleton.
SH-RP83.

Raymond Pallier – The Hound of the Baskervilles (15/19). 29th Jan 1922

Images 5/5. Page 56. Dr. Watson and Sherlock Holmes talk about the case and how Holmes had been on the moor watching events.
SH-RP84.

Raymond Pallier – The Hound of the Baskervilles (16/19). 5th Feb 1922

Images 1/6. Page 67. This illustration is clearly in the wrong place, not only is he later shown collecting food and clothing from John Barrymore, but he has yet to fall from the hill.
SH-RP85.

Raymond Pallier – The Hound of the Baskervilles (16/19). 5th Feb 1922

Images 2/6. Page 67. Sherlock Holmes (He managed to bring a couple of coats down to Dartmoor.)
SH-RP86.

Raymond Pallier – The Hound of the Baskervilles (16/19). 5th Feb 1922

Images 3/6. Page 67. John Barrymore hands over food and clothing to the Convict Selden, who just happens to be His brother-in-law.
SH-RP87.

Raymond Pallier – The Hound of the Baskervilles (16/19). 5th Feb 1922

Images 4/6. Page 67. Jack Stapleton arrives to view the body of Selden. *SH-RP88.*

Raymond Pallier – The Hound of the Baskervilles (16/19). 5th Feb 1922

Images 5/6. Page 68. The convict Selden falls off the cliff after being chased by the Hound. (a death much anticipated in earlier images)
SH-RP89.

Raymond Pallier – The Hound of the Baskervilles (16/19). 5th Feb 1922

Images 6/6. Page 68. Jack Stapleton meets up with Dr. Watson and Sherlock Holmes on the moor and discovers the dead body of the convict Selden *SH-RP90.*

Raymond Pallier – The Hound of the Baskervilles (17/19). 12th Feb 1922

Images 1/5. Page 79. Sir Henry is told about the events on the moor and the death of the convict Selden.
SH-RP91.

Raymond Pallier – The Hound of the Baskervilles (17/19). 12th Feb 1922

Images 2/5. Page 79. Sir Henry Baskerville is told that there is nothing to fear now.
SH-RP92.

Raymond Pallier – The Hound of the Baskervilles (17/19). 12th Feb 1922

Images 3/5. Page 79. Sherlock Holmes shows that there is a similarity between Sir Hugo Baskerville and one of the local people. Clearly there is a hidden Baskerville in the area.
SH-RP93.

Raymond Pallier – The Hound of the Baskervilles (17/19). 12th Feb 1922

Images 4/5. Page 80. Sir Henry Baskerville says goodbye to Sherlock Holmes, who is returning to London.
SH-RP94.

Raymond Pallier – The Hound of the Baskervilles (17/19). 12th Feb 1922

Images 5/5. Page 80. Sherlock Holmes and Dr. Watson prepare to travel back to London at the Railway station, but they aren't really going anywhere. *SH-RP95.*

Raymond Pallier – The Hound of the Baskervilles (18/19). 19th Feb 1922

Images 1/6. Page 91. Laura Lyons is visited by Holmes and Watson and reveals all.
SH-RP96.

Raymond Pallier – The Hound of the Baskervilles (18/19). 19th Feb 1922

Images 2/6. Page 91. Inspector Lestrade arrives at the Railway station to be greeted by Holmes and Watson. He is carrying an arrest warrant.
SH-RP97.

Raymond Pallier – The Hound of the Baskervilles (18/19). 19th Feb 1922

Images 3/6. Page 91. Inspector Lestrade, Dr. Watson and Sherlock Holmes travel to the moor to await events that evening.
SH-RP98.

Raymond Pallier – The Hound of the Baskervilles (18/19). 19th Feb 1922

Images 4/6. Page 91Sherlock Holmes paying the driver and telling him to return to Coombe Tracey.
SH-RP99.

Raymond Pallier – The Hound of the Baskervilles (18/19). 19th Feb 1922

Images 5/6. Page 92. Inspector Lestrade, Holmes and Watson wait for Sir Henry Baskerville to leave Merripit house heading for home.
SH-RP100.

Raymond Pallier – The Hound of the Baskervilles (18/19). 19th Feb 1922

Images 6/6. Page 92 Holmes listens for the sound of Sir Henry Baskerville walking back home to his hall.
SH-R101.

Raymond Pallier – The Hound of the Baskervilles (19/19). 26th Feb 1922

Images 1/7. Page 103. A hound it was, an enormous coal-black hound, but not such a hound as mortal eyes have ever seen. Fire burst from its open mouth, its eyes glowed with a smouldering glare, its muzzle and hackles and dewlap were outlined in flickering flame. Never in the delirious dream of a disordered brain could anything more savage, more appalling, more hellish, be conceived than that dark form and savage face which broke upon us out of the wall of fog.*SH-RP102.*

Raymond Pallier – The Hound of the Baskervilles (19/19). 26th Feb 1922

Images 2/7. Page 103. The Hound is killed and Sir Henry Baskerville is saved.
SH-RP103.

Raymond Pallier – The Hound of the Baskervilles (19/19). 26th Feb 1922

Images 3/7. Page 103. Sir Henry Baskerville recovers from the shock of his encounter with the Hound.
SH-RP104.

Raymond Pallier – The Hound of the Baskervilles (19/19). 26th Feb 1922

Images 4/7. Page 104. The fate that would await Jack Stapleton if he was captured.
SH-RP105.

Raymond Pallier – The Hound of the Baskervilles (19/19). 26th Feb 1922

Images 5/7. Page 104. Beryl Stapleton lead the group in a search for her husband Jack Stapleton.
SH-RP106.

Raymond Pallier – The Hound of the Baskervilles (19/19). 26th Feb 1922

Images 6/7. Page 104. Holmes recovers Sir Henry Baskerville's stolen boot discarded by Jack Stapleton.
SH-RP107.

Raymond Pallier – The Hound of the Baskervilles (19/19). 26th Feb 1922

Images 7/7. Page 104. The final fate of Jack Stapleton.
SH-RP108.

You are looking in the wrong book if you want these illustrations.

Volume 1 index

Doyle, Charles Altamont 17
Doyle, Charles– A Study in Scarlet 18
Friston, David Henry 21
Friston, David Henry - A Study in Scarlet 22
Greig James – A Study in Scarlet. 1895 27
Greig, James 26
Greig, James – A Study in Scarlet 1896 28
Paget, Sidney Edward 29
Paget, Walter Stanley 394
Sidney Paget – A Scandal in Bohemia 31
Sidney Paget – The Adventure of Abbey Grange 378
Sidney Paget – The Adventure of Dying Detective 395
Sidney Paget – The Adventure of Second Stain 386
Sidney Paget – The Adventure of Silver Blaze 135
Sidney Paget – The Adventure of the 'Gloria Scott' 166
Sidney Paget – The Adventure of the Beryl Coronet 117
Sidney Paget – The Adventure of Black Peter 334
Sidney Paget – The Adventure of the Blue Carbuncle 84
Sidney Paget – The Adventure of the Cardboard Box 144
Sidney Paget – The Adventure of the Charles Augustus Milverton. 341
Sidney Paget – The Adventure of the Copper Beeches 126
Sidney Paget – The Adventure of the Crooked Man 188
Sidney Paget – The Adventure of the Dancing Men 309
Sidney Paget – The Adventure of the Empty House 295
Sidney Paget – The Adventure of the Engineer's Thumb 101
Sidney Paget – The Adventure of the Final Problem 226
Sidney Paget – The Adventure of the Golden Pince-Nez 361
Sidney Paget – The Adventure of the Greek Interpreter 202
Sidney Paget – The Adventure of the Missing Three-Quarter 370
Sidney Paget – The Adventure of the Musgrave Ritual 173
Sidney Paget – The Adventure of the Navel Treaty (1/2) 210
Sidney Paget – The Adventure of the Navel Treaty (2/2) 219
Sidney Paget – The Adventure of the Noble Bachelor 109
Sidney Paget – The Adventure of the Norwood Builder 302
Sidney Paget – The Adventure of the Priory School 324
Sidney Paget – The Adventure of the Reigate Squire 179
Sidney Paget – The Adventure of the Resident Patient 195
Sidney Paget – The Adventure of the Six Napoleons 347
Sidney Paget – The Adventure of the Solitary Cyclist 317

Sidney Paget – The Adventure of the Speckled Band 92
Sidney Paget – The Adventure of the Stockbroker's Clerk 159
Sidney Paget – The Adventure of the Three Students 354
Sidney Paget – The Adventure of the Yellow Face 152
Sidney Paget – The Boscombe Valley Mystery... 58
Sidney Paget – The Case of Identity 51
Sidney Paget – The Five Orange Pips 68
Sidney Paget – The Hound of the Baskerville (1/9) 235
Sidney Paget – The Hound of the Baskerville (2/9) 242
Sidney Paget – The Hound of the Baskerville (3/9) 250
Sidney Paget – The Hound of the Baskerville (4/9) 257
Sidney Paget – The Hound of the Baskerville (5/9) 264
Sidney Paget – The Hound of the Baskerville (6/9) 270
Sidney Paget – The Hound of the Baskerville (7/9) 277
Sidney Paget – The Hound of the Baskerville (8/9) 281
Sidney Paget – The Hound of the Baskerville (9/9) 288
Sidney Paget – The Man with the Twisted Lip.. 74
Sidney Paget – The Red-Headed League 41
The Bristol Observer 8
The Bristol Observer – A Study in Scarlet 13
The Bristol Observer - The Sign of Four Story 9

Now this is a handy reference, isn't it?

Canon Opus, Code and Title

No.	Code	Name
1	STUD	A Study in Scarlet
2	SIGN	The Sign of (the) Four
3	SCAN	A Scandal in Bohemia
4	REDH	The Red-Headed League
5	IDEN	The Case of Identity
6	BOSC	The Boscombe Valley Mystery
7	FIVE	The Five Orange Pips
8	TWIS	The Man with the Twisted Lip
9	BLUE	The Blue Carbuncle
10	SPEC	The Speckled Band
11	ENGR	The Engineer's Thumb
12	NOBL	The Noble Bachelor
13	BERY	The Beryl Coronet
14	COPP	The Copper Beeches
15	SILV	Silver Blaze
16	CARD	The Cardboard Box
17	YELL	The Yellow Face
18	STOC	The Stockbroker's Clerk
19	GLOR	The Gloria Scott
20	MUSG	The Musgrave Ritual
21	REIG	The Reigate Squire
22	CROO	The Crooked Man
23	RESI	The Resident Patient
24	GREE	The Greek Interpreter
25	NAVA	The Naval Treaty
26	FINA	The Final Problem
27	HOUN	The Hound of the Baskervilles
28	EMPT	The Empty House
29	NORW	The Norwood Builder
30	DANC	The Dancing Men

No.	Code	Name
31	SOLI	The Solitary Cyclist
32	PRIO	The Priory School
33	BLAC	Black Peter
34	CHAS	Charles Augustus Milverton
35	SIXN	The Six Napoleons
36	3STU	The Three Students
37	GOLD	The Golden Pince-Nez
38	MISS	The Missing Three-Quarter
39	ABBE	The Abbey Grange
40	SECO	The Second Stain
41	WIST	Wisteria Lodge
42	BRUC	The Bruce-Partington Plans
43	DEVI	The Devil's Foot
44	REDC	The Red Circle
45	LADY	Lady Frances Carfax
46	DYIN	The Dying Detective
47	VALL	The Valley of Fear
48	LAST	His Last Bow
49	MAZA	The Mazarine Stone
50	THOR	Thor Bridge
51	CREE	The Creeping Man
52	SUSS	The Sussex Vampire
53	3GAR	The Three Garridebs
54	ILLU	The Illustrious Client
55	3GAB	The three Gables
56	BLAN	The Blanched Soldier
57	LION	The Lion's Mane
58	RETI	The Retired Colourman
59	VEIL	The Veiled Lodger
60	SHOS	Shoscombe Old Place

Quick reference to illustrators in this volume

No	Code	GG	RG	GWH	TJN	RP	AT
1	STUD	3	24				1
2	SIGN	1	24	42	33		
3	SCAN	1	5				
4	REDH	1	4				
5	IDEN		3				
6	BOSC		4				
7	FIVE		3				
8	TWIS		5				
9	BLUE		5				
10	SPEC		5				
11	ENGR		4				
12	NOBL		4				
13	BERY		4				
14	COPP		5				
15	SILV		6				
16	CARD		4				
17	YELL		3				
18	STOC		4				
19	GLOR		3				
20	MUSG		4				
21	REIG		5				
22	CROO		4				
23	RESI		5				
24	GREE		3				
25	NAVA		9				
26	FINA		5				
27	HOUN		30			114	
28	EMPT		3				
29	NORW		3				
30	DANC		3				

No	Code	GG	RG	GWH	TJN	RP	AT
31	SOLI		3				
32	PRIO		3				
33	BLAC		3				
34	CHAS		4				
35	SIXN		3				
36	3STU		4				
37	GOLD		4				
38	MISS		4				
39	ABBE		3				
40	SECO		3				
41	WIST						10
42	BRUC						6
43	DEVI						
44	REDC						
45	LADY						
46	DYIN						
47	VALL						
48	LAST						
49	MAZA						
50	THOR						
51	CREE						
52	SUSS						
53	3GAR						
54	ILLU						
55	3GAB						
56	BLAN						
57	LION						
58	RETI						
59	VEIL						
60	SHOS						

GG – Graham Grinham
RG - Richard Gutschmidt
GWH – George Wylie Hutchinson
TJN – Thomas Jeffs Nicholl
RP – Raymond Pallier
AT – Arthur Twidle

www.ingramcontent.com/pod-product-compliance
Lightning Source LLC
Chambersburg PA
CBHW081134300726
48982CB00005B/959
* 9 7 8 1 7 8 7 0 5 9 2 5 2 *